D1736885

1

Brandon Berntson
When We Were Dragons

Cover art by www.derangeddoctordesigns.com

Join the mailing list and get updates at
www.brandonberntson.com

when we were dragons

BRANDON BERNTSON

For Shaylyn and Taylor,
Lucas and Jacob,
Kennadi Reese, and Jude Love
Magical children, all.
Though most are no longer children.

1.

The Collision

We came here a long time ago when we were dragons. There were a lot of us then before our worlds collided: Lane, Murrochoe, and the Old Ones.

My name is Justin Silas. I'm from Amberlye, an eastern city on Paramis, and I'm a dragon. I know what you're thinking: How can a dragon talk, let alone, write? Your legends concerning dragons, of course, are not the same as ours.

Dragons have two identities on Paramis. Although we don't appear human, we have human forms. In my mortal form, I, Justin Silas of Amberlye, stand at seven feet, two inches tall. My skin is reptilian. My dark red eyes (so I've been told)—to mortals—look evil, but I assure you, I'm a gentle giant. Random patches of scales splotch my skin. Two hooked protrusions—hints of wings—are visible on my back under my shoulder blades. My wings aren't fully exposed or completely visible until I change. My skin is a fiery mix of orange, red, and black. Karen says I'm a walking conflagration as opposed to her bright, shimmering lilac and blue. I have jet-black hair, which somehow—still unexplained to us—disappears when we change. We carry no weapons, but we breathe a blistering cloud of fire.

I've read similar tales concerning your folklore. There is the legend of Nu Kua in China, a goddess who mothered dragons who could shift from mortal to dragon form. They could soar to the highest heavens or the deepest oceans. This is similar to our kind, though we're not born from goddesses.

Dragons on Paramis are born from fire.

According to the western world (where we ended up), dragons were terrible beasts. We were considered manifestations of evil but also guardians of treasure. The people of Earth say they'd never seen a dragon until we came along except in picture books and movies, yet there are legends concerning our kind. We're not monsters, not all of us. Many of us are guardians, but not of treasure.

We are watchers and protectors.

Life here is more technologically advanced than what we're used to. Gadgets, gizmos, and trinkets of all kinds baffle me to no end. I puzzle over them endlessly, trying to figure out how they work. After the collision of Earth and Paramis, these gadgets stopped working altogether. Things became more primitive.

Our people, a mix of men, women, children, dragons, and Old Ones, aren't ruled by a single government. They grow their own crops and live off the land. There is trade aplenty. We have a barter system based on abundance and need. Where there is a need, abundance is meted out. It's simple. Our people, much like Earth, are content with agriculture and trade.

We have large harbors, countless ships, and teeming cities. The Old Ones enforce the laws, which come from Cerras, our one and only God. The Old Ones keep to themselves and are rarely seen except by dragons.

Powerful forces were at work on Paramis before the collision— Lane's doing, a traitor to our kind. She had discovered a dark magic, trying to tap into Cerras' power. Once the collision happened, something was different about us. Something was different about the people of Earth as well. Karen mentioned it to me shortly afterward:

"It's as if I can feel who I am, but I'm a stranger to myself as well. I don't understand it, Justin. I've never felt this way before."

Karen is a beautiful, tall, and graceful dragon, slightly shorter than my seven-feet two inches. She has powder blue skin and black eyes with jet-black hair. Karen has a gentle, quiet acceptance about her I admire. She never gets angry and never raises her voice. She's always calm and sensible in the face of danger, and she is light years ahead of me.

I do not possess her patient quality.

I met Karen in the city of Delayne, a western city on the continent of Mandabelle. Karen has a knack for telling stories, and children flock to her from all around to hear her weave strange, sometimes true, sometimes fictitious yarns. I've seen hundreds of children sitting around her at one time, staring with wide, unblinking eyes while she embellished tales of the Old Ones, dragons, and men.

But I knew what she was talking about . . .

I was a stranger to myself as well.

It was a soulless, aimless time on Paramis before the collision. Everyone was restless. Cerras slept, and Lane was plotting. The people of Earth felt much the same. Or so I've been told. They were anticipating a strange, colossal event.

Afterward, they seemed energized, as though some bright light hovered beneath their skin. Not all of them owned it, but it reminded me of Dilla-Dale and the Old Ones—scholars, sages, and wizards from Paramis.

The answers eluded us. *We* were the magical ones, were we not? Earth had never, as far as we were concerned, owned such power.

But I wondered . . .

Magic on this planet was nothing more than an illusion, a form of deception and trickery. The names Harry Houdini, David Copperfield, among others, propped up on occasion, but they were mere charlatans. The magic on Paramis was *not* trickery.

It was real.

The collision combined both worlds, Paramis and Earth, as ridiculous as that seemed. Sacrifices were made. The event, strangely enough, wasn't as catastrophic as you might think. There were casualties. Many people lost their lives, but it could've been worse. While the collision shook and wiped out Earth's modern conveniences, Paramis also suffered a depletion of its magic. Other forces were at work. Both worlds were spared major destruction, and instead, experienced a sort of . . . merging.

Vestiges of both worlds are intertwined with each other now. Canastelle is still an icy region to the north of Amberlye, towering glaciers that look like giant blue Popsicles jutting into the sky. The Forests of Glammis, haunted woodlands, are also here. Rumors say Glammis breeds fairy-folk and elves, but most of those stories—like your dragon legends on Earth—are the stuff of fairy tales.

Amberlye, a modest city on the edge of the eastern sea, is no longer here. I miss it terribly. There is Delayne, where Karen is from, another teeming port, larger than Amberlye. I could go on and on about Paramis, but we'd be here a while.

And I have a story to tell.

According to your scientists, the collision was an impossible event. It should've never happened, not without ramifications and catastrophes on both sides, which there were, but it should've been worse. Much worse.

It wasn't.

I thank Cerras for that. Earth should've dropped from its orbit, sending the entire planet into a frozen tailspin, wiping out all life. The same should've happened to Paramis.

The reason both worlds survived is simple.

It was the power of Cerras.

Or magic; however you want to look at it.

Somehow, in ways the Old Ones aren't aware, Earth and Paramis had fused together, making one very strange, unordinary planet.

Electricity is still in use in some places, but it's selective. Vehicles are accessible if you can find gasoline and a car with all its moving parts, but most people travel by bike or horse these days. Roads lead to abrupt dead ends of grass and walls of towering rock. To the naked eye, it's a strange, colorful, versatile, bewildering place, yet extraordinarily unique and beautiful at the same time. The modern technology of Earth merged with the magic of Paramis. For a while, they seemed to cancel each other out.

We learned quickly this wasn't so.

The collision claimed many lives. It happened during the year 6133 on Paramis, which was around 2024 on Earth.

I was walking hand in hand with Karen when it happened. We love to fly together in our dragon forms, but on this particular day, we were strolling hand in hand along the Coralie River, near the Mountains of LaSie.

Everything went black—the moon and the stars. Screams sounded from nearby villages. Confusion and chaos shook the world apart. The ground writhed violently underneath us.

"Justin!" Karen cried.

Clouds swarmed with vicious speeds across the skies. Something extraordinary but horrifying was happening, and we had no idea what it was.

I kept hold of Karen's hand for as long as I was able.

The sky turned a molten, muddy, blood color. The stars—as miraculous as it seemed—fell from the sky, swirling and tumbling together. The collision was like a giant god holding one world in each hand, then smashing them together. In a way, I wondered if it was true. A myriad of blue lights arranged themselves in the night sky, then dispersed like rocket-fire. Lightning flickered behind clouds. A rumble shook the firmament.

"Maybe this is the end of our world," I told her, with finality.

The ground loosened, swallowing villages, houses, and buildings. Then something miraculous happened . . .

Another shift took place. Everything merged back together, reforming, reshaping, restructuring the land into a melting pot of abstract houses, trees, mountains, villages, cars, trucks, roads, and buildings. What came out was something like a complex piece of worldly art on a universal grand scale.

I lost contact with Karen, my hand falling away.

When I awoke, strange creations dotted the land.

Paramis and Earth were one.

Massive hunks of metal, wheels, headlights on, not driving on the road, but partly submerged by grass and dirt. These strange, man-made configurations—cars, motorbikes, houses, and telephone poles—had become part of the land in their own unique, haphazard way. Car horns sounded until the batteries died. Trees grew from slabs of concrete. Concrete shined with the glow of lights that had somehow been embedded underneath. Automobiles and motorbikes merged with wood, water, and stone. I didn't know what any of these things were. I was seeing it all for the first time and asked many questions later. Paramis, our home, had been invaded by ancient relics from an unknown land.

Both worlds were still intact for the most part, and although there were casualties, many had survived. We didn't know about Earth, not until later. We were still trying to figure out what had happened. *We* were alive, most of us, two completely different races separated by galaxies and stars, light years beyond our own comprehension . . . the other side of the universe. Yet we'd never been so far from home.

Magic, or the power of Cerras, had brought us to another galaxy. We'd collided with another world. We had not been knocked out of orbit, nor had Earth. We'd merged, been remade, and suffered losses on both sides. We lived on a single planet with two vastly different races, beliefs, customs, and philosophies. Many weren't happy about it.

New things merged with the old, combining wood with steel, rock with plastic with all the assortments and accouterments you could think of. To say the collision had disrupted the land, well . . . that's what the Earthlings call, 'an understatement.'

Cars and trucks had sunk into the earth, grills matted with soil, twigs, and grass growing from chrome and tires. Telephone poles, streetlights—all gone or strangely altered—were a mixture of rock, wood, and steel. It perplexed, allured, confounded, and stretched the imagination.

A once asphalt intersection was now a grassy knoll with streetlights suspended over it by two elm trees. Twigs and branches with meshed aluminum and wood remade a stop sign. Comically, the white paint spelled the S and the T, while twigs and leaves made the O and the P. Crystals and gems replaced metal streetlamps, sending auroras of natural light in all directions instead of the illumination from electricity and light bulbs.

During the collision, the stars—swirling and falling from the sky—hovered inches above the ground, huge white balls of silvery brilliance lighting up the neighborhoods, villages, and cities. You couldn't look at them for long without needing to shield your eyes. While some hovered inches off the ground, others were high in the air next to rooftops and trees. Stars come in all shapes and sizes. Maybe these were stars of a different kind, a light sent from Cerras to illuminate this newer world. Some were as small as golf balls, others the size of large vehicles. They never stayed in the same place. They like to move around at night, as if trying to return to their places in the sky.

Stars are now scattered across New Earth and Paramis Altered.

Roads traveled for blocks or miles until they ended in a wall of boulders or a mountainside. Some roads ended in a copse of aspen or pine trees, rivers, or large bodies of water. It was all very astounding.

Ancient, gnarled trees from Paramis meshed with steel beams and metal framework, making half-trees and bizarre, leafy-looking structures. Windows in houses had turned to leaves. Leaves turned to sparkling glass. The silver grill of a car emerged from the bole of a tree down the block, but strangely, the rest of the car had disappeared.

What happened to the forest and rivers, the Mountains of LaSie, where we'd been walking moments ago? Where was the Coralie River? Was this a dream? Who were these people around us wearing strange, alien garb?

If you've never seen a dragon before, the sight is not pleasant, at least not to the people of the Earth. Even though we hadn't transformed into our dragon forms, we were frightening to look upon. That's what Karen and I first experienced.

People fled, panicked, in all directions. Someone threw a rock at me, clipping the side of my head, drawing blood, and sending me— as quickly as I had come out of unconsciousness—into darkness again.

When I awoke a second time, I shook my head, slightly woozy, and decided to look for Karen. I prayed she was still alive.

The screaming continued. Confusion and noise added to the pain in my head. Some people were being attended to. Dragons as well. People from both worlds administered treatment while others yelled and screamed in horror. I was trying to place who these people were. They looked no different than the men and women on Paramis, but they were clothed in ways I'd never seen.

How long had I been under? I blinked several times, smelling smoke. One second, I'd been strolling with Karen under the Mountains of LaSie; the next, it was pandemonium.

A loud, painful ringing sounded in my ears. My head throbbed from the rock someone had thrown. Despite feeling woozy, I trudged on.

I spotted Karen under a large pine tree, electrical wires hanging from the branches. Christmas lights blinked on and off. I would learn later that we had come to Earth at a festive time of year.

Her chest rose and fell. She was lying on her side, one arm covering her face. She was alive, and I hurried over, kneeling down, and gently shook her powder blue shoulder. Leaves and twigs were stuck in her raven black hair.

"Karen," I said. "Are you okay?"

She stirred and rolled onto her back. Her eyes fluttered, opened, and focused on me. Karen has the same shade of eyes as her powder blue skin. They looked like ice.

"Justin?" she said.

"Hey there, pretty lady."

She blinked several times, sat up, and grabbed her head. "What happened?"

"I don't know," I said. "Be careful. Are you hurt?"

She shook her head. "I don't think so, just . . . stunned."

I helped her to her feet, and the fog seemed to clear. Together, we took in our new surroundings, along with the bedlam.

Karen looked at the strange configurations of buildings, houses, trees, and cars fused together, making the most ludicrous structures you'd ever seen. The important thing was we were alive, but our lives and the lives of the people around us would never be the same.

The sky was molten, reddish black. The clouds were thick, charcoal-colored with scarlet tendrils woven underneath. The wind carried the smell of fire and rain.

"We should find some of the others," Karen said. "I hope Gill is okay."

I nodded, agreeing. Gill was her brother, whom we hadn't seen in some time. He was usually off on one of his adventures and would visit when he got around to it. Gill could never tolerate standing in one place for very long.

We walked cautiously through the streets and hills, a strange mixture of neighborhoods, forests, mountains, asphalt, and stoplights, looking for familiar faces, the Old Ones, anyone. We kept clear of the panic-stricken. For all we knew, they'd think *we* were the cause of this madness, lynch us, hang us, or execute us in some bizarre, torturous ritual that defined dragons as the hellish beasts we were.

Someone had to have an explanation.

—

We found Dilla-dale after roughly two hours. It's hard to find your own kind when you have to hide from would-be attackers. We spent more time dodging rocks and gunfire than anything.

Dilla-dale wasn't the first familiar face we'd run into. Humans fled from dragons who were trying to instill order, endeavoring to placate the denizens of Earth while trying to persuade them we weren't harmful, despite our sinister appearances. You can imagine the results. Dragons trying to pacify humans? You had to see it to believe it. We would have to sort out the confusion later, instill order of some kind, but that wasn't going to happen anytime soon.

Trying to ignore all this (as Dilla-dale was doing), we found one of the Old Ones rummaging through a pile of fallen stones, trying to unearth his buried library one book at a time. It was the remains of

15

his precious tower. All the Old Ones have one. The towers spot Paramis here and there like lonely, isolated structures. Here, the ancient ones peruse—for days on end—the mysteries of magic, gods, and the universe. A stack of dusty tomes was piled next to him on the ground. Dilla-dale was filthy and disoriented from trying to gather them all up—along with the collision.

"Dilla-dale," I said.

Four-hundred and some odd years old, the man looked no older than forty. He wore a long dusty robe that had been brilliantly white at one time but had faded to a dingy yellow. He had long, thick brown hair and deep blue eyes, a sharp, chiseled face, and a broad chin. The hood of the robe was off, exposing his grimy face. He stood up after setting several books aside and seemed relieved to see us.

"Justin," he said. "Karen. Thank Cerras, you're okay."

He embraced us, and we hugged him in return.

"Have you seen any of the others?" I asked.

Dilla-dale shook his head.

In the distance, a large towering mountainside took up most of the sky. Screaming was audible from a distance, people shouting. A gunshot cracked in the air, and all three of us winced at the report.

"This is crazy," Karen said, looking around, as though we might be ambushed any minute.

"There are casualties on both sides," Dilla-dale said, nodding. "I'm afraid some of the Old Ones have perished along with dragons. People from both sides."

Dilla-dale, despite the atrocities, seemed strangely calm.

"I think this is all I'm going to salvage from this ruin," he said, looking at his books.

I knew he loved his tower. Seeing it in a pile of rubble pained not only him but me as well. He leaned over and grabbed several books. Karen and I helped, carrying the larger tomes. Dilla-dale looked around and heaved a sigh. He looked at me, then at Karen.

"It's happened," he said. "I didn't know it would. I don't think any of us knew. Or we didn't quite believe it. Cerras has plans."

"Cerras?"

"Perhaps the Sleeping God is no longer asleep," he said.

This only confused me.

"Excuse me?" I asked.

"The collision," he said. "As it was written."

"Written. Since when? Where?"

Apparently, the Old Ones kept secrets from dragons as well.

"Come on," he said. "Let's go find some of the others, and I'll explain."

Walking from the ruins of his tower, we went in search of other dragons, sticking to the shadows of strange, towering trees, the three of us carrying an armload of books.

The wind blew the scent of death and fire from the north, the clouds thicker, blacker overhead. With the scent came the smell of rain, and it was soon coming down hard.

I spread my wings over the books, trying to keep them dry, and we made our way across unfamiliar terrain.

2.
A Giant Made of Amber Quartz

The sky was a thick blanket of dark red clouds, pelting our faces with rain. I asked Dilla-dale to hand me the books he was carrying since he was wingless, and they were getting wet.

A strange, burning smell was in the air. It was the twisting, smoldering metal from the collision. Mixed with the rain, it made a warm, coppery aroma. The belly of the clouds was also a strange, fiery illumination, as if mirroring the conflagrations on the ground.

We found Cullen Markel, Lila of Percival, and Louis of Olivette, all dragons, looking as scared and confused as Karen, Dilla-dale, and I.

Cullen had wounded his arm during the collision. He sat, dazed, his back against a tree intertwined with metal. A large gash bled, stretching from his shoulder to his elbow. His head was bleeding, too, a copious flow of dark blood covering the side of his indigo face. Lila, a beautiful yellow dragon with silvery hair, tended to his wounds with strips of cloth she'd found. They looked relieved to see us, and the same feeling must've shown on our faces.

In the intervals, I still remember the humans fleeing in terror, unable to comprehend what we were. Once I thought about it, I couldn't blame them. Their planet was in turmoil, and strange monsters were suddenly everywhere.

I shook my head, weighed by the pressure and impossibility of my thoughts. I had a feeling the world had yet to undergo further horrors. I was thinking too much as always, and it wasn't doing a bit of good.

"Cullen?" Karen asked, bending toward the indigo dragon.

"He'll be okay," Lila said. "He was flying during the blackout."

"Head's a little fuzzy," Cullen said, clenching his eyes and putting a hand to his brow.

"I think he just likes a lady to take care of him," Louis said, smiling.

Cullen opened his eyes and frowned at Louis. "Always the comedian," he said.

After we got Cullen to his feet, he shook off the worst, and we retreated to an abandoned barn at a nearby farmhouse. Horses ran wild outside. Inside, bales of hay towered to the rafters. Louis, who is a dark purple dragon, found some wood. Lila and I cleared a large spot for a fire, making a slight depression in the dirt, and cleared away most of the hay. After Louis returned, he set some logs in the pit and breathed slightly on the wood, drying them out from the rain. The logs sparked to life and caught, and we sat in a circle around the crackling flames. From outside, hovering stars sent rays of light through the cracks in the walls and roof. A white glow from the stars and the orange fire illuminated everyone's faces in a sinister glow. I could only imagine what sort of devil I must look like with my cauldron-colored skin and black eyebrows.

"Where are the rest of the Old Ones?" Cullen asked. Silvery, dark blue hair matched his skin, pointed ears rising through his hair. His eyes were an eerie color of lavender, which made him look intimidating, along with his deep, baritone voice. He had an intense look on his face, but I attributed that to the wounds he'd suffered.

"I don't know," Dilla-dale said. "We tend to go our separate ways at times. Loners of the same order, so to speak. Most of us don't even know where the others live."

That was true. Dilla-dale and the others had always worked alone, except when some new wisdom needed to be shared. The collision was obviously an exception.

"Dilla-dale is the loneliest loner of the Old Ones," I said, smiling.

He nodded. "Murrochoe, more so," he said. "But I do tend to steer in my own direction. Even though I have *you* to look after."

We all chuckled, then were silent for a while before Karen looked up, playing with strands of hay.

"Cerras," she said.

It wasn't a question, and for a brief second, I saw a dangerous showdown in the future, an evil premonition of things to come.

Dilla-dale agreed, and what we heard next was a brief history lesson (or part of one) of Paramis. We knew most of it, but the Old Ones had kept certain details to themselves.

"Cerras wasn't the first of the Old Ones," he said. "He is the father of us all. He made the wind, the stars, the trees, and the world we know as Paramis. He made other worlds as well. Earth might be part of that. Who knows? We'll have to ask some of the leaders here if we can find them. But we'll worry about that later.

"The history of Cerras has many gaps. No one knows how old he is. Or how long Paramis stood silent before he breathed life into it. There are legends that say he walked for centuries alone, examining every detail of the land, taking delight in his own creation. If you want to talk about loners, Justin, Cerras is a man—or god, if you will—who revels in solitude. I think he prefers his own company to that of others. No one enjoys the silence of nature more or spending time in his own creation the way Cerras does. I believe it's one of his greatest joys.

"Once he'd created the worlds, he decided to sleep and let things run their course. In that time, mortals, dragons, the Old Ones came to be. The Old Ones followed his teachings, and he wrote his laws upon our hearts. It's why we were made to rule. I guess we're more like saints, you could say. Sometimes, we can hear the Sleeping God speaking to us as we pray. You may have heard of him referred to as the Giant God, as well.

"When he was done with his creation, he walked toward the frozen regions of Canastelle. For miles, he traveled into the deepest, iciest caverns, lay on a sheet of ice and rock, and willed himself to sleep."

"You mean, he willed himself to *die?*" Cullen asked, holding his arm.

"Only in a manner of speaking," Dilla-dale said. "He never woke up, or *hasn't,* not up to this point. That we *do* know. He could wake any time he wanted. Obviously. Maybe now is one of those times. As it was—or *is*—his body hardened, turning to quartz and other precious gems . . . or so I hear. No one has actually ventured into those caves, let alone found his body. His physical nature is the energy and magic of Paramis. Cerras is the crux of all life and magic from men, women, children, the Old Ones, and dragons. From him, all matter is sustained. He enforces the laws of both spirit and nature. What would you expect from a god?"

Glances were exchanged all around.

"So, he really is a giant?" Lila asked. "A sleeping giant?"

Dilla-dale looked at her and nodded. "A giant made of amber quartz," he told her.

21

I bit my tongue and almost burst out laughing. A giant made of amber quartz? Was he serious? I didn't know whether to laugh or cry. Our planet was a fairy tale, sure, and despite its history, we'd never heard all the details of this particular story. I knew he'd gone to sleep but . . . amber quartz? That seemed a bit dramatic.

"So, how did the collision occur?" I asked.

Dilla-dale looked at me. "I believe it was Lane," he said, simply. "I believe she has somehow tapped into the power of Cerras and willed the collision."

I furrowed my brows. Karen took my hand, squeezing it. I squeezed hers in return.

"But that's impossible," Louis said, his indigo skin turning a shade darker. "Lane doesn't have that kind of power."

"She does now," Dilla-dale said. "There are legends in old books, some of them here in the ones Justin and Karen helped me salvage." He patted the tomes next to him. "The Eyes of Cerras are very powerful and, apparently, removable."

"Excuse me?" I asked.

Dilla-dale looked at me and nodded. "It's true, Justin. And there are shadows. Shadows with secrets, who know things we do not. There is great power in the Eye of Cerras. And if Lane, who we all know is a traitor, has access to these shadows, she could have information we do not. She may know exactly where the Sleeping God lies."

He paused for a bit and said, "You've heard of Tor-Latress?"

I laughed out loud, more like a scoff. I'd never believed in Tor-Latress. I thought he was a myth, nothing more than shadow, the product of gods and fairy tales, but I was being educated about our own history in a way I never had before.

Dilla-dale looked at me with disappointment.

"You're kidding me, right?" I asked.

He shook his head. "Tor-Latress, Justin, is very real. The stories of his existence have been exaggerated, sure, but they're not far from the truth.

"I think Lane extracted the Eye. That's what caused the collision—or Cerras decreed it to happen for reasons we don't know yet."

I shook my head. Tor-Latress. Half spirit, half shadow, made of pure evil. He had come into being, or so the myths had told us, from a brother of Cerras born from darkness.

"But Lane couldn't have extracted the Eye without help," Karen said. "Even Tor-Latress couldn't have helped her do it. Who else did she use?"

"That's what we're trying to find out," Dilla-dale said. "She used someone or something. But it couldn't have been anyone from Paramis. Paramis doesn't have that kind of magic."

I looked at him for a long time. Then my eyes went wide. "Do you think it was someone from here?" I said. "From *this* planet?"

Dilla-dale took a deep breath and nodded. "I think that's exactly what happened."

I let out a breath and felt my heart gallop.

Karen squeezed my hand again.

—

"So, what does Lane plan on doing with the Eye?" Lila asked.

The fire was dwindling. The stars moved back and forth outside, sending light through the gaps in the barn walls. The rain stopped, and we sat huddled around the flames, thinking of two worlds torn apart, then brought together again.

"Rule. Dominate. Rip the worlds apart again," Dilla-dale said and shrugged. "I don't know. The power of Cerras might be enough to do that."

"You mean she'd send both worlds into chaos again?" Cullen asked. "What could she possibly hope to gain?"

Dilla-dale looked at him. "Lane, like any tyrant, madman—or madwoman—in this case, thrives on power and destruction. She despises her own kind: dragons, the Old Ones, even humans. She has always been that way. To her, we're all weak, and dragons have their own destiny. It has nothing to do with gods or the Old Ones. My guess is she'll allow the chaos and confusion to go on for as long as possible. There's already bedlam, and that satisfies her. She might—as crazy as it sounds—try to destroy Cerras completely with his own power.

"Remember, she was banished for killing her own kind. She retreated to Canastelle, perhaps to find Cerras' body. Lane longs to rewrite the pages of history, and she believes she can do it. She longs to sit upon the throne of creation with the dead god at her feet with Tor-Latress as her advisor. Lane's mad enough to believe she can do it. What more could she do with the Eye than create the ultimate chaos, send worlds colliding into one another again? But for a different reason. I think the collision was only the beginning."

"So, we have to find Lane," Cullen said.

"Not as easy as it sounds," Dilla-dale said. "You forget about Tor-Latress. And with the Eye, who could stop them?"

"This is insane!" Louis said, his features hardening.

"So, what are we supposed to do?" Lila asked. "Sit back and watch her destroy two worlds altogether?"

Dilla-dale shrugged. "I don't know," he said. "But we have to find the others. More importantly, the Old Ones."

No one said anything.

The rain started again, beating on the roof of the barn.

—

After a time, the rain stopped, and we put out the fire, walking outside into the misty evening. It was quiet. Whatever had happened throughout that first day, people had found solace in hiding places or accepted this strange turn of events—at least for the time being. The looting, terror, and whatever it was around us had calmed. It was a bizarre world, whether we wanted to believe it or not.

We went our separate ways, none of us sure where we were going, but we promised to stay close. Dilla-dale set out to find more of our kind. Cullen, Louis, and Lila followed him, providing protection more than anything. Karen and I headed in the opposite direction, trying to accept the changes, along with all we'd heard.

Karen grabbed my hand and looked at me. "Things are never going to be the same again, are they?" she asked.

"I don't think so," I said.

I didn't like that prospect at all. But what choice did we have? Paramis wasn't our home anymore. We had other people to think about now. Here was an entirely new breed of folk. Were they terrified, awed, shocked, revolted by what they saw?

My thoughts turned to Lane, hypnotic, alluring Lane, in all her evil green skin, red-haired, and yellow-eyed beauty. Lane was one of the few dragons who carried a weapon, a law strictly forbidden on Paramis. It was a long-handled saber. We were dragons. What did we need weapons for?

I closed my eyes. For some reason, I couldn't stop thinking about Lane. I wanted to focus on what was happening. I wanted to focus on Karen.

We didn't know where we were going. It was getting late. The wind picked up with a cold breeze. What had once been neighborhoods was now a jigsaw puzzle with missing pieces.

"Look," Karen said.

Ahead of us, a woman with three children—two girls and a boy—stood wet from the rain. They had stunned looks on their faces, standing in front of a house. The house had sunk into the ground. The only thing visible was the porch, the front door, and the eave turned upwards, facing the sky. The rest of the house had been swallowed by the earth.

The woman wore a bright red shirt with long sleeves. The kids wore similar clothes; the two girls had sweatshirts on, pants made of thick, blue fabric. The boy wore a black t-shirt with the number 17 written on it in yellow. Upon closer inspection, I saw the woman had tears in her eyes, holding a hand to her face.

Not knowing what they might think, Karen and I stepped closer, taking our chances they might not be frightened of us.

Oddly enough, it was the most natural thing in the world, approaching these strangers from across the galaxy. Looking back, I see how that encounter became the turning point of our lives—all of us.

The children turned and looked at Karen and me. The woman, the mother, opened her eyes wide as we approached: one powder-blue dragon, one red demon. The mother's hair was in a ponytail. Her face was round and healthy with a clear complexion.

Maybe it wasn't shock but a kind of awe. The boy smiled at us. He had thick brown hair (wet because of the rain) and big dark eyes, a cherubic face. The girls had long, straight brown hair, matching their mother's.

They'd seen others like us already, so maybe it didn't surprise them. Maybe the initial shock had worn off. As I looked at the ruin,

I realized it must've been their home. Someone very close to them had been lost in the collision.

The mother was speechless. I couldn't blame her. The girls looked back and forth between Karen and I, and I saw the resemblance between the four of them.

"Your house?" Karen asked.

The woman nodded.

I'm often stunned by what should've been a massive language barrier. Despite where we were from, we spoke the same language. I wondered if this was Cerras' doing as well.

"Mom?" the boy asked. "Was Dad still in there?"

I made a silent vow to Lane and Tor-Latress. Watching this family and thinking about Lane brought out the wrathful side of me. I could barely contain it.

The woman replied the only way she knew how. I felt a tug at my breast. How was she going to explain it? From the looks on the girls' faces, I knew they understood what had happened.

"I . . . I think so, Charlie," his mother said.

"Dad," the boy said in a feeble voice, looking at the house, and began to cry.

"Is there anything we can do?" Karen asked.

The woman looked at her, wishing we *could* do something. Reverse time, prevent any of this from happening. Give them back their father. It was a useless statement, a hopeless statement, but it was the only one Karen knew.

The woman shrugged. "We were taking a walk while he was . . . making a surprise dessert for us, and then . . ." She shook her head. Tears filled her eyes.

"Mom," the taller girl said, putting her hand on her arm.

We could find her a home, someplace warm, and get them fed. It wasn't an offer, but it was the best I could do. The only way to make sense of the collision was to start mending things as soon as possible. That's exactly what I wanted to do with this woman and her children.

I walked up, putting out my hand, which seemed the oddest thing in the world. "Justin Silas of Amberlye. This is Karen of Delayne. We're from Paramis."

The woman's eyes grew larger. The tension and grief disappeared, if only for a moment. She looked like she was about to cry again. This was a strong woman, a nurturing, beautiful woman who lived for her family, and her family had just been torn apart.

"Paramis?" she said.

"Our world," I said. Her hand was soft but cold. She didn't want to let go, despite my massive red paw. "Before our worlds collided."

"Collided?" she asked, seeming to grow more frustrated. These words meant nothing to her.

Poor woman, I thought. Lost husband, lost house, strange, talking dragons towering over her. What next?

"I don't know all the details myself," I said. "There was a collision, some strange event on both worlds. Somehow our worlds came together."

She let go of my hand and introduced herself:

"I'm Holly Underhill," she said. "These are my children: Charlie," she said, indicating the boy, "Jody," the shorter, younger girl, "and Mellicent."

"Sorry we had to meet under such circumstances," Karen said.

The woman nodded and turned back to the house.

Two races of people from light-years apart, standing together in a very awkward, very confusing moment. Despite the tragedy, there was something special happening here.

"We should find a place for you to stay, at least for now," I said.

Holly nodded, and I noticed Charlie looking at us in awe.

"What *are* you?" he asked.

Jody and Mellicent raised their eyebrows. I looked at them and tried to smile without scaring them.

"Charlie," Holly said. "That's not polite."

"It's okay," I said. I looked down at Charlie, a small boy, his eyes brimming with wonder, large and curious.

"We're dragons," I said, kneeling to his level. Charlie's eyes grew wider.

"But you don't have *wings,*" he said.

Karen laughed beside me.

"Not at present," I said. "Only when we need them."

Charlie looked perplexed, then smiled.

"I'll show you sometime," I said. "Okay?"

"Cooool," he said, and that seemed to be the end of it.

We left the ruined structure in search of a new home for Holly and her children.

We found her a house in a newer, suburban development, a white, modern structure, two-stories high. The place was called Aspen Groves. It was one of those neighborhoods that was still under development. Not all the houses had been finished yet. But it was one of many places that hadn't been affected by the collision, which was fortunate. Other families were taking note and doing the same, finding a place to stay with the loss of their homes.

It was a big, empty place without furniture, larger than what they needed, but a fireplace in the living room made it attractive. There was plenty of room for all of us. I went in search of some logs, came back with an armload, and set them on the hearth, positioning them in the fireplace. Not realizing what I was doing, I leaned over and breathed on them, setting them on fire. Charlie was watching this from behind me, and he jumped up and down with excitement.

"Wow! Wow!" he cried. *"Do it again! Do it again!"*

I shook my head.

"If I do it again," I said. "I'll set the whole house on fire."

Karen and I decided to roam around a bit. Holly wanted to go with us, so we left Mellicent to watch after the kids, and we got our first taste of modern America. Holly mentioned some items they could use, describing them to me and where we could find them.

At a nearby department store, Items For Less, which was being heavily ransacked, we found some pillows, sleeping bags, and some canned and dried food to get them through the next few days. I realized we were breaking the law, even with the house we'd found them, but I also knew things had changed since the collision. We didn't have much choice. People from our world and Earth moved in and out of the store, filling grocery carts, helping one another. I was baffled by this already, but I also knew it wasn't happening everywhere.

Batteries, flashlights, lamps, food, water, propane, stoves, clothes, and other sundry items were being shared. In some strange way, they were coming together, at least in this part of town.

Many of them ignored us for the most part, too busy with their own needs. Maybe they realized we were harmless since none of us attacked or made trouble, or since Holly was with us. Everyone was more concerned with their own needs.

One old man, wearing a black and red-checkered hat, nodded at us and said, "Better get what you can before it's gone. Nice to meet you, folks." Karen and I exchanged a bewildered glance and shrugged. Holly nodded and said thanks.

We had too much stuff to carry, so we simply pushed the carts all the way back to Holly's house. I marveled at the simplicity of the shopping cart, how these people produced food, clothing, and other items to fulfill their needs. We learned later that we were in a place called Broomfield, Colorado, a town of roughly 30,000 with a view of the Rocky Mountains to the west. A shadow of LaSie was visible in those mountains, making them taller and more majestic.

The kids were grateful to see us when we came back. After we put everything away—most of it dry goods because the refrigerator was inoperable—we sat on the floor of the living room and lit several candles. Mellicent, Jody, and Charlie munched from a box of crackers, spreading cheese onto each one. Holly said we'd arrived a month before Christmas and that snow had been on the ground before the collision, but all the snow had disappeared. I told her it was summer on Paramis during the collision, and it must've— with the two seasons—settled for spring because it was warm outside.

"So, what's Paramis?" Holly asked. A mindless look crossed her face, trying to register what had happened: her husband gone, she and her children forced to live in a strange, incredulous world.

"Paramis is a primitive land peopled by mortals, Old Ones, and dragons."

"You don't *look* like dragons," Charlie said.

Mellicent and Jody looked at Karen and me in wonder.

"We can shift," I said.

"Like a transformation?" Holly asked.

I nodded. "I'd do it, but I don't want to scare the children."

"I want to see you shift!" Charlie said, excitedly.

Mellicent and Jody smiled at Charlie.

"Maybe later," I said.

Charlie looked crestfallen.

"So, what happens now?" Holly asked.

I looked at her for a long time, shook my head, and thought about how I was going to answer. I didn't have an answer. I didn't want to mention Lane or Tor-Latress in front of the kids.

I shrugged. "Find a way to get things working again," I said. "The Old Ones will figure something out."

Charlie broke the thought with an observation: "So, there are *more* dragons?" he asked.

I nodded. "Many more," I said, smiling. "But we're not harmful."

A lie, I realized, thinking of Lane.

I looked at Karen. She seemed to share the same thought.

"We're not scaring you, are we?" I asked.

I thought back to the barn, our meeting around the fire, and how devilish Louis and Cullen had looked, how evil I must've appeared with my cauldron-colored skin, thick black hair, and black nails in the candlelight. How could I *not* terrify them?

"No," Holly said, sounding unconvinced. "It's just . . . I don't know . . . amazing. It's hard to believe. I keep thinking I'm going to wake up, that none of this is happening. But . . . it's just too real. I'm *aware* of how real it is. I just . . . don't know how this could've happened."

I looked at her, a beautiful, healthy woman. I saw her for who she was: strong but sensitive, vulnerable but resilient. On the surface, she was a fearless mother who would sacrifice whatever she had to for her children. Harm *had* befallen them; it had taken her husband. Since Karen and I arrived, she and the children said no more about it, and whatever pain she felt—along with the kids—they kept to themselves. When I looked at her, she seemed on the verge of losing control again. I could tell she needed some time to accept and process what had happened. We all did.

"There's only one way it *could've* happened," I said.

They looked at me, eyebrows raised.

"Magic," I said.

I expected them to scoff, but they didn't. Charlie smiled wide. How else did it explain the world around us? He looked at Holly.

"See, Mom," he said as if that explained everything.

Holly smiled, the first genuine smile I'd seen all night. The thought seemed to please her.

Holly still thought about her husband, I assumed, wondering why the magic hadn't saved him. She confirmed it a second later, voicing it aloud without realizing: "Couldn't save him," she mumbled.

There were tears in her eyes. She noticed me looking at her.

Karen went to Holly and put her arm around her shoulders. Holly responded and threw her arms around Karen, sobbing quietly into her chest. Karen whispered some words of comfort and eventually pulled away.

"Mom," Charlie said. "Are you all right?"

Mellicent was quick to give the perfect answer:

"Mom's just glad we found someone to take care of us, Charlie," she said. I looked at her, surprised by her sagacity. Mellicent looked at me, smiled, and I nodded a single time.

Holly pulled away from Karen and apologized.

"Don't be silly," Karen told her.

Holly wiped her eyes with both hands. She tried to smile, and her beauty hit me all at once. I'd never seen a woman look as beautiful through grief as Holly did at that moment. She had dignity and reserve, and I felt an immense wave of responsibility for them, the reason for our origin perhaps. I understood exactly why we'd met them and what we were here for. I wanted to take care of them. For some bizarre reason, I felt a powerful loyalty to these four people, and Karen felt the same.

Hours ago, we'd woken from darkness, confused, bewildered, and scared. Already, I was anxious to put my life on the line for Holly and her children. It was strange, something I didn't understand, but I didn't have to. It was the way we were made. Like Dilla-dale had said.

We were protectors.

I loved Karen deeply, and I would give my life for her, but I'd never felt such a surge of paternal love as I did for Holly and her children then. It hurt and surprised me at the same time. It still does—even as I write this. It was the first day on this new world, and a lot had happened already. We weren't dragons, breached by time and space, worlds away in forgotten lands. Holly and her children were no different than the rest of us. It was confounding, wonderful, and beautiful all at once.

In the span of hours, two completely different beings had come together.

But with Holly and her children, we'd found something more precious than gold.

We'd found a family.

3.
Coming Together

I missed Paramis terribly in the short time we'd been here, the Forests of Glammis, the Mountains of LaSie. More importantly, I missed Amberlye, my own city on the shores where the Old Ones had found me. Dilla-dale said I was a pup of a dragon then. He likes to bring it up, trying to make me feel infantile.

"Barely hatched from the egg," he'd say. Not finding much humor in the statement, I would glare at him with my red eyes and send a few puffs of smoke in his direction.

"Touchy," Dilla-dale said.

I missed the architecture: towers, thatched cottages, villages and towns, even the muddy streets. When I looked around at this new world and saw only remnants of our citadels—massive stone formations emerging from the boles of trees or embedded into the mountainsides—I grew emotional and longed for home. Earth was more intact, more its own world, whereas Paramis seemed to disappear altogether in some places, leaving only hints of its existence. It made me sad in many ways. Where were the cities, the kingdoms, the primitive regions devoid of technology, open spaces of nature, mountains, rivers, oceans, and trees? I could fly for hours looking at the land unfolding below me, the span of oceans, and how wide and endless they seemed.

But the land had changed, and it would never be the same again.

I missed the festivals and celebrations, the banquet halls in palaces where men, women, dragons, and Old Ones would gather to dine, dance, mingle, and celebrate a new year, holidays, special events, even birthdays. The only thing separating Paramis from Earth was the technology—now gone, most of it anyway. I'd never seen anything so strange as these bulky, hulking cruisers on wheels moving seemingly on their own: cars, trucks, and motorcycles.

I missed soaring over vast glaciers in my dragon form, the frozen landscapes of Canastelle, flying through the cold air, and marveling over the world Cerras had made.

I wondered what kind of devils had been unleashed here, if any, and what we were about to discover. A newer, darker evil suddenly *not* Earth but from Paramis?

I wondered what Lane and Tor-Latress had in mind.

After a week, Dilla-dale and Earth's—or I should say, America's leaders—came together to organize a rally. Dilla-dale, Lila, Cullen, and Louis succeeded in tracking them down. They talked about the situation on—what we'd come to think of as—New Earth and Paramis Altered. Despite the skepticism, as news traveled throughout the nation, they'd arranged a gathering consisting of Earth's denizens and the people of Paramis.

Talks ensued on both sides.

The clouds, after a week, finally parted, revealing a bright blue sky. The chill in the air had mixed with summer on Paramis, and the temperature was warmer than expected. All this was surprising after the collision, but I knew it had to be the result of Cerras. The god was taking care of everyone while still trying to put the world back together.

For a week, fliers publicized the event, plastered on trees, telephone poles, and street signs. Trucks drove along roads and half roads, grassy knolls, wherever they could go, men announcing from bullhorns: *"Meeting between Paramis and Earth! Meeting between Paramis and Earth!"*

I couldn't help thinking how amusing all this was, even comical. You had to see it to believe it. Everyone and their families—from dragons to men were asked to attend.

The rally took place at Broomfield Community Park, a large patch of flat grass. The turnout was enormous. During the collision, the park—because of magic—had been reconfigured strangely with the courthouse, a long structure with stone pillars, and plenty of windows. Tree branches wove throughout the stonework. Some of the windows were made from grass and leaves. I was still trying to wrap my brain around these strange configurations.

Thousands of people showed. Fountain drinks, hot dogs, hamburgers, nachos were available at various stands throughout the park. I'd never seen anything like it.

"It's like the amusement park, Mom," Charlie said.

Holly looked down at him and smiled.

"What's an amusement park?" I asked Holly.

35

"A place people go to be amused, silly," Karen said.

"You've been developing quite the sense of humor," I told her.

Karen shrugged. "I think it's this New Earth," she said. "I kinda like it."

Mankind from Earth and dragons stood side by side.

Dilla-dale and a man named Preston Montgomery, the Vice President of the United States, Rudy Granger, the mayor of Broomfield, along with the help of others, had organized the rally. If anything, maybe this would bring some clarity and peace.

Preston was an agreeable man, much to the relief of many dragons, an open-minded individual, willing to accept the changes that had occurred. What choice did we have? The collision had killed the President of the United States, and Preston was now America's spokesman, while Dilla-dale spoke for Paramis.

Cars and trucks lined the perimeters. A huge throng of men, women, dragons, and children gathered for the event. It was all very colorful. A bandstand had been erected. Since there was no electricity, at least not yet, bullhorns were used instead of microphones.

The facts were self-evident. Neither world had been prepared for such a life-altering, cataclysmic event, but living together—sorting through the wreckage, finding peace, and coming together—was our only option. Neither world meant the other harm. Differences would have to be set aside. Someone compared it to the racial divide America had undergone during the sixties. From what I'd heard, that area was still tricky to navigate. Dragons and Old Ones, someone shouted out, should live on one half of the planet while the people from Earth occupied the other. Mention was made of destroying all dragons because we were nothing more than monsters.

"This isn't the dark ages! Go back where you came from!"

"You have wings!" someone shouted. "Fly home!"

The argument was how, in the past, segregation had created more harm than good. It had only made things worse. Hadn't we learned anything?

"These aren't people! They're monsters!" someone else shouted.

"But we've come too far to resort to such primitive thinking!" Preston shouted.

Within minutes, it was pandemonium.

Pick-up trucks brimming with angry citizens carrying chains, baseball bats, and rifles showed. Gunshots rang through the air.

"Please! Please! People! Remain calm! This is exactly what we're trying to avoid!" Preston looked frantic and frustrated.

"We didn't come here of our own free will to overtake your world!" Dilla-dale tried to placate the crowd through a bullhorn. *"We're just as confused as you are. We mean no harm. Our dragons are here to help you, to protect you! You see them standing there! We're all in this together! Please, we need to have order! We need a civilized society, and we can make that happen if we all come together!"*

When dealing with magic, not all of Earth agreed. Dragons breathed fire. How did they know we weren't going to create more destruction? Look around, they shouted. The Old Ones were immortal. The people of Earth were afraid we would enslave them, take over their world. Things had already changed. Proof of that was everywhere. On Paramis, we'd never faced this kind of problem before. Earth and its people wouldn't listen to dragons, the Old Ones, let alone their Vice President. Thankfully, not everyone agreed. Many were willing to give it a try.

Because of it, a rebellion ensued. Shouts and jeers claimed *we* were the result of the collision, that *we* had made it happen.

"Go back where you came from!" someone shouted.

Dragons can be quite intimidating. A cold stare is enough to make one's point, but in this case, we would have to try harder. For a second, I thought of sending out a cloud of flame, a mighty roar to get everyone's attention, but I knew that would only make things worse.

Holly and her children stood side-by-side with Karen and me behind them. How could we live peacefully when so many were unwilling to cooperate? Holly and the kids were proof others felt the same. We had to use this to our advantage, lead by example if we were going to make it work. I thought about the man I'd seen at the department store who'd treated us as equals. We were no different; we were *not* monsters. We would have to rebuild society and enforce new laws. We had no choice. Preston and Dilla-dale returned to these issues emphatically, but to no avail.

The mob had other ideas.

I thought about Lane. No doubt, she was close at hand, a smile on her pale, green face, yellow cat eyes peering over the crowd. Tor-Latress, his shadowy wings, hovered at her shoulder.

Dilla-dale, several dragons (Louis and Cullen among them), and four men of Earth's government, including Preston Montgomery, stood before the crowd. What a colorful mix of men, women, and dragons! Rudy Granger, Broomfield's mayor, was a tall, brown-skinned man with a deep, booming voice. He spoke through a bullhorn of his own:

"If I could have your attention, please! Attention, please! Everybody! We're not accomplishing anything!"

The crowd, after some time, managed to calm down.

"Revelations have come to us all," Granger continued. *"I've been appalled by the crimes I've witnessed. For those of you criminals, laws are still and will be enforced. Police are still on duty. There has been looting and thievery. I understand the collision has destroyed families and homes and that we need food, shelter, and clothing in order to survive. We have encountered an incredible change. We have provided caravans to help those in need. But rest assured . . . any crimes committed will result in punishment. We are newcomers to dragons and the Old Ones, just as they are newcomers to us. They did nothing to set these events in motion, and we will not bring them harm. We can set a good example, make them feel at home!"*

"How do you know?" someone shouted. *"They're pulling the wool over your eyes, mayor!"*

Rumblings, stirrings through the crowd.

"Please! Please!" Granger paused. Silence followed. He nodded a single time and spoke through the bullhorn again:

"Our worlds are not the same! And there is nothing we can do about it! Nothing! Enough lives have already been lost. But we still have a world to live in. We still have friends and families. We're still alive! We're foreigners to them, just as they are foreigners to us. Ill will, rancor, and hate will not be tolerated! This is as much their world as it is ours. We have no choice but to live with one another, to help those in need, and come together as men, women, dragons, and Old Ones. For that to happen, we need to show some compassion and empathy! It's vital to our survival! Compassion and empathy will help us overcome our differences! We need to help

each other and rebuild a working community again. Please! 'Love thy neighbor as thyself!' That includes dragons and Old Ones!"

Many of Earth's denizens refused to see things this way. People dispersed, walking away, shaking their heads, taking their families with them.

"Traitors!" one man screamed from the back. "Look what's happened to our world!"

"Nothing has happened to our world that hasn't happened to theirs!" Granger tried to point out. *"Rebellion won't accomplish anything! We're better people than that! We've battled this over decades among our own kind. We cannot start the same decline again. Let's prove to the Old Ones and the dragons that we're a tolerant, open-minded people, a loving, compassionate race of men, women, and children, that we can share our world and our homes, just as they can share their knowledge and their magic with us. Imagine what we could learn from one another! Imagine the opportunity for growth we have before us! We cannot be quick to judge or make assumptions about our neighbors. We grow by hearing their stories, by learning who they are, why they believe and live the way they do. Who are we to decide? This is not a catastrophe! People, it's a blessing! It's an opportunity to move forward and grow as a new race of men, women, children, dragons, and Old Ones!"*

Shouts of praise echoed over the thousands. Cheers erupted with a deafening roar. I had to admit, after Granger's speech, I felt a tug of emotion, one I hadn't thought about before. Perhaps I was just as guilty and scared of the people of Earth as they were of us. I was amazed the rest of the world, Earth, hadn't taken to this man's philosophy, but it had been well played, whether he meant it or not. Those words, though not resonating with everyone, resonated well enough with many. To those it did, we remained standing side-by-side.

I felt a shred of hope. I looked around and saw many nodding, dragons, men, women alike, smiling at one another, as if to say, "Of course, why *wouldn't* we want progress? We can do this." I saw men and dragons immersed in something I'd never imagined before. Those remaining behind were anxious to start a new life. For those who'd lost loved ones, it was easy to blame us for those losses. If we could've prevented it, we would have. That was obvious. Many others felt the same. Holly didn't blame us for the death of her husband. She was willing to accept the change, despite how difficult it would be.

"We are facing trying times ahead!" Granger reminded us. *"The Old Ones have confirmed a greater threat. If we don't come together to battle this evil, we'll be worse off than we are now. Think of your wives and children! Think of the state of our society! We have no choice! Please! Everyone! People and dragons! We must live in peace!"*

Cheers all around, but others followed the throng of non-believers, wanting nothing to do with it. Trucks backed up and peeled out of the area, bats and rifles held high.

Just as quickly, it got ugly. From nowhere, shouts drowned out Granger's pleas. Rocks and bottles showered the bandstand. Earth's people were angry. A wave of pity surged inside me for these uninformed creatures, people unwilling to share their world and lives with ours. It was like watching a bunch of greedy kids fight over a meaningless toy.

Stones flew through the air. Someone clipped Granger on the side of the face with a rock. He fell to the stage, holding his hand to his jaw. Dilla-dale moved toward him, trying to protect him. He grabbed Granger by the arm and pulled him off the stage. Preston took the bullhorn and tried to calm the crowd, but it was too late.

Our first attempt at bringing people and dragons together had failed. Was there another way? What else could we have done?

Some shouted and claimed dragons *could* protect them. We were a blessing, but any hope to coerce them turned to more insults, jeers, and violence. I was proud to see every dragon spreading its wings as the debris flew, holding their wings in front of innocent bystanders.

We had to get Holly and the children out of there. As quickly as we could, we spread our wings without transforming completely, shielding them as the others had done. Charlie, Mellicent, and Jody were more in awe of our massive wings than of the riot.

Later, through town, I remembered seeing a sign that read: *Dilla-dale for President!* Another read, *The Dragons Have Arrived!* I turned to these things as signs of hope, but it was short-lived. Homes were set on fire. The looting continued. Hadn't there been enough destruction already?

Luckily, Preston and Granger had organized a band of police officers with shields and tear-gas in case of such an emergency. After several hours, with clouds of smoke covering the park, the crowds dispersed. The worst casualties were several concussions, some broken bones, and some minor injuries.

Some of the people turned to Lane's side. No doubt, she reiterated their beliefs: we were harmful and must be destroyed. I could only imagine how pleased she must've been watching this unfold.

Some shouted they didn't need leaders anymore, let alone dragons. They'd fend for themselves.

Despite the collision and the horror to follow, a war between Earth and Paramis seemed inevitable, which Granger and Dilla-dale had been trying to avoid since the beginning.

We checked on Dilla-dale, Preston, and Granger. Granger was bleeding from his jaw, but the wound wasn't deep. The rock had taken off a layer of skin. Their faces mirrored my thoughts. It seemed hopeless.

"I'm afraid I haven't represented the people very well," Granger said.

"It's not your fault," Dilla-dale said. "We were fools to think a few speeches would bridge the gap between two vastly different beings. Dear Cerras, we're practically alien races to each other, and suddenly we're forced to coexist, whether we want to or not. For now, it's best to let things simmer down. We'll figure something out."

"Are you okay, Rudy?" Preston asked.

Granger tried to smile, touching his head lightly, and said, "So much for politics."

"Maybe that's the problem," Dilla-dale said.

Surprising us, Granger and Preston laughed. Dilla-dale looked at Holly and the kids.

"You seem to have made some friends," he said.

"Dilla-dale," Karen said. "This is Holly Underhill, Charlie, Mellicent, and Jody. We met several days ago. But we thought we'd watch over them for a while."

Dilla-dale cocked his head and looked at Charlie. A strange expression crossed his face. "Hello, young man," he said.

Charlie stuck his hand out, the perfect gentleman. They shook. "What's up, dude?" he said, grinning.

Dilla-dale seemed at a loss for words and couldn't reply. The rest of us were quiet. Dilla-dale frowned at Charlie, then looked at me. "I think this is just what we need, Justin," he said. "Lead by example. Watching over Holly and her kids might be just the thing we need, proof we mean no harm by protecting each other."

I nodded, agreeing.

Before we parted, I noticed Dilla-dale sneaking another glance at Charlie. I had no idea what was going through his mind and reminded myself to ask him about it later.

—

I failed to mention something else when we were in the barn before we met Holly and the kids. There was more to that conversation:

"Murrochoe," Dilla-dale had said, "thinks Cerras has an enemy."

Murrochoe, unlike Dilla-dale, looked his age, roughly seven-hundred or thereabouts. He had long silver hair and green eyes, but no one had seen him since the collision. There was also Karen's brother, Gill, whom we still hadn't seen, and whom Karen was beginning to worry about. Karen grew restless with his absence. We assumed he'd have found us by now, but no such luck.

"You mean, besides Lane and Tor-Latress?" I asked.

He nodded. "A twin. An opposite. Cerras' brother."

"Why do I feel like I should've known that?" Lila said and shook her head.

Dilla-dale sighed and rubbed his hand across his brow. "There is mention of his name in some of the old records, but it's never been proven. I'm afraid many of the myths and fairy tales of our planet are not myths *or* fairy tales."

He paused and rubbed his chin. "We're at a disadvantage," he said. "We have to find Lane. I never thought the Eye of Cerras held that much power, but apparently, Lane knows something we don't."

"What do you suggest?" Cullen asked.

"Dragons," Dilla-dale said. "We have to get all the dragons together we can and search the land. We have to look for any sign of Lane."

All of us were quick to volunteer.

"That's admirable," Dilla-dale said. "A few of you will have to stay behind. Dragons can cover a lot of ground in a short time, but some will have to come with me."

"Why do you want some of us here?" Cullen asked. "The more dragons in the sky, the quicker we'll find Lane."

Dilla-dale looked at Cullen for a long time. "I need some of you to remain behind for obvious reasons," Dilla-dale said.

I raised my eyebrows.

Dilla-dale sighed, frustrated, as if it were obvious. "I need you to remain behind because I'm worried about the people from Earth," he said. "I need you to protect us."

———

When we got back to Holly's house, a noticeable change had taken place around the neighborhood. Many of the 'fallen stars' had shifted again. They never stayed in the same place for long. Every day a different part of the neighborhood brightened with their changing illumination. Some of the stars rose high into the air as if realizing they belonged to the sky.

The stars, however, weren't the reason for the change.

People had gathered, apparently organizing things of their own. People and dragons covered every lawn, trucks moving in and through the makeshift streets of asphalt and grass. Trucks carried furniture, boxes of food, clothing, and various supplies. After the rally, it was a hopeful sight.

Despite everything we'd experienced, some had come together instead of rebelling. They decided their community, their neighbors, and their lives and the world were worth saving. I felt a surge of emotion for these creatures and how they'd banded together. Various dragons moved alongside them, helping move furniture, clothes, and food into their homes. I'd never seen people coming together as I did then.

"Wow," Holly said.

We stopped, taking it all in.

"Looks like we got some neighbors, Mom," Jody said.

"Maybe Granger's speech was more effective than we thought," Mellicent said.

Karen was beaming. "I think I'm gonna start crying," she said.

I couldn't believe how busy the neighborhood was. After several days of confusion, the sight of the vehicles, people, and dragons in the brisk warm air gave me hope . . . even if that hope seemed limited.

"AHOY THERE!"

A man shouted to us from a large yellow moving van with the word *Penske* written on the side. He wore a black sailor's cap. An unlit cigar was pinched between his teeth. "Where do you want it?" he asked.

We looked at one another. I shrugged.

"Excuse me?" Holly asked.

"Where do you want it?" he asked again. He had a bristly face with silver and black whiskers. He was everything nautical. If I didn't know any better, I'd say I was looking at a sailor from Paramis. His arms were thick, bulbous, and bronzed from the sun.

Holly looked at me, waiting for instruction. I shrugged and held my palms up. "Accepting gratuities is half of being charitable," I said.

Holly smiled. I thought she was going to cry. Her eyes glossed over. She walked over to the man, leaving us near the pathway toward the house. I looked around, watching the neighborhood.

"These mortals are a very surprising people," Karen said next to me.

I nodded. I didn't mention my cynicism as to how half of them were just as eager to lynch us.

The man and Holly exchanged a few words. Holly laughed and wiped tears from her eyes. The man laughed as well. They talked for several minutes before Holly came back. The man put the truck in gear and backed into the driveway.

"It appears we have some furniture, new clothes, *and* more food," Holly said.

"Wow," Charlie said. "I get to sleep in a *bed* tonight? That kicks crocodile pants!"

"We *all* get to sleep in a bed tonight, ya goof," Mellicent said.

Charlie rolled his eyes and stuck his tongue out at his sister.

Karen and I looked at each other. We walked over to where the man was backing the truck into the driveway of Holly's new home. With all of us helping, it didn't take long to unload it. There were three beds for the four of them, but Mellicent didn't mind sharing one with her sister, she said. Karen and I said it was okay to go without beds because of our height. Rugs were a step up in the world compared to cold cave floors.

The man, whose name was Jonathan Mokkell, said he was going back into town for more supplies. Several other trucks dropped off various items throughout the day: barbecue grills, clothes, food, sleeping bags, blankets, first aid kits, anything and everything you could think of to put the neighborhood back together again.

I thought about the collision and what had happened. I thought about worlds merging, how most of the supply stores were—fortunately—still intact.

During the move-in, Holly couldn't stop crying. It was quite a spectacle. She'd stop for a minute and laugh, then start crying again.

"Gosh," she exclaimed. "I'm sorry. I don't know why I'm acting like a big, dumb baby."

"You're not a big, dumb baby," I told her.

"But I *feel* like a big, dumb baby," she said.

Karen started laughing. Mellicent and Jody joined in. Charlie seemed a trifle confused by all the emotion, as if moving into a new home should be more a reason to laugh than cry. I stood there, soaking it all in, feeling emotional myself, like . . . well . . . like a big, dumb baby.

—

We helped Holly organize the house. Another truck arrived, and we helped unload more supplies. The truck was full of mattresses and clothes. For some bizarre reason, the plumbing had come on recently. Holly's house and others along the neighborhood, surprisingly, had hot water. There had been several plumbers earlier making the rounds, from what the neighbors had told us. There was also an electrician in the area that was rewiring all the houses, rerouting everything to a local grid system, which was connected to a local power plant. I didn't understand how any of this worked, let alone what it was, but he had an entire crew to help with the process. I was amazed by their technology. It was a form of magic I'd never seen before.

I thought of Cerras and wondered if he was smiling in his sleep.

On Paramis, the water is always cold unless you heat it over a fire. I stepped into the bathroom, feeling the hot streams against my palm. "Karen," I said. "Come and feel this."

She put her hand in the shower, feeling the streams, and raised her eyebrows. "That is very odd," she said. "How do you think they do it?"

"Is it magic?" I asked.

"I think it's called a water heater," Holly said, smiling. "Do you mind if I take a shower now?"

Embarrassed, we exited the bathroom.

Holly wanted to take advantage of this right away since she hadn't been able to wash since the collision. She took a long, hot shower, coming out smelling of soap, bristling bright and new, and wearing fresh, clean clothes. The kids took turns as well. They were very excited to take a shower. I'd never seen people so excited to be clean. As it was, once darkness fell, enough lights outside from the shifting stars illuminated not only the neighborhood but the inside of every house as well.

Later, after snacks and a dinner consisting of peanut butter and banana sandwiches, potato chips, and blackberry soda, Charlie stood up and said, "Hey everybody! Wanna see a magic trick?"

"Magic trick?" I asked, somewhat stunned. I wasn't aware magic existed on Earth, at least in the way we understood on Paramis.

Charlie nodded eagerly, his eyes bright and wide. He held a blue handkerchief the color of Karen's skin. "Ready?" he asked.

"Anticipating every moment," I said.

Charlie smiled and threw the handkerchief above his head. It fell slowly through the air and over his hand. He pulled the ends of the handkerchief tightly over his fist, and just as quickly, pulled it away. In his hand was a bundle of vivid red roses. They were real. I could smell them from where I stood.

I looked at him, amazed. My mouth hung open stupidly. I didn't know what to say. I didn't know what to *think*. Jody, Holly, and Mellicent gasped in surprise. Karen clapped as if the act hadn't surprised her at all.

"These are for you, Karen," Charlie said, handing her the roses.

Karen was overcome. She took a deep breath. It's hard to admit, but I was touched.

"Thank you, Charlie," she said, her voice thick.

Charlie beamed, turned, and bolted up the stairs as if embarrassed. We turned and watched his tiny figure disappear out of sight.

Holly stared at the roses in wonder. "I don't . . . I mean," she tried to say. "I've never seen him do that before."

"That was *amazing,*" Jody said, with awe in her voice.

"Look, Mom," Mellicent said. "They're real."

"Why wouldn't they be real?" I asked.

Karen leaned in and inhaled the roses. They weren't a predictable, plastic substitute like most magicians used (at least that's what Holly explained to me later). The roses were real, soft and silky to the touch. I bent to inhale the scent and see for myself.

Magic? I thought. What was going on here? Had Earth always been in possession of magic? Charlie's trick wasn't a masterful illusion, but it was still authentic.

The more I thought about it, the more I realized Charlie didn't *look* like the Charlie I'd encountered a week before. Before he'd performed his trick, I noticed a radiant hue emanating from deep within, as if one of the 'fallen stars' had buried itself beneath his flesh. Maybe they weren't 'ordinary' people anymore. Maybe more was going on here than I suspected. Maybe the collision had changed everyone in a way we hadn't anticipated, let alone imagined.

In the days to follow, I would see that magic for what it was.

—

Later that night, at roughly 2:30 in the morning, I awoke on the living room floor.

I opened my eyes, stretched, and sat up, looking out the living room window. One of the stars, the size of a microwave oven, hovered outside, throwing a silvery blue glow into the room.

I heard a sound from upstairs and turned my head. Someone was crying. I stood up, my head almost grazing the ceiling. I made my way upstairs, holding the banister, the steps creaking under my weight.

The crying grew louder. One of the children, I thought?

I made it to the top of the stairs, walked down the hallway, and cocked my head. I put my ear to the door the sound was coming from.

It was Holly's room.

I knocked lightly to warn her, grabbed the knob, and opened the door. I peeked inside and winced.

The room was ablaze with light. I was virtually blinded. A star hovered outside Holly's window, similar to the one downstairs, only brighter and much larger. It felt like standing on the sun.

I looked at Holly, shielding my hand over my eyes, and said her name. She looked up, embarrassed. This poor girl had been crying a lot lately, and I could only imagine what she must be feeling.

"Holly?" I asked. "Are you okay?"

She waved me inside, motioning me to shut the door. I did as she asked and went to the bed, sitting on the edge. Bent in half, I was still taller than she was. I put my hand on the blanket where her knee was. Holly smiled through her tears. What a pretty woman, I thought—probably thirty-five. Without the tears, she looked ten years younger.

"I just saw Carl," she said.

I didn't know who Carl was. I'd never asked, and I'd never had the chance. I remembered when Karen and I had met Holly and the kids, so it wasn't hard to figure out who Carl was.

"I know you miss him," I said.

She looked at me. Her eyes were big and brown, Charlie's eyes. She shook her head.

"No," she said. "Carl. He was *here.*"

I wasn't hearing her correctly. I looked at her, unable to comprehend. I frowned, then began to worry. I was hoping our precious Holly wasn't losing her mind.

She looked at me again and tried to smile. Tears fell from her eyes, making wet tracks down her cheeks.

"Carl was . . . *here?"* I asked.

She nodded vigorously. "I woke up because that ball of light was right outside the window. It was so bright." She looked at the ball of silvery-blue light, which made her skin look like electric marble. Her eyes were black pools of ink. She turned and looked at me again. "He was standing by the window," she said. "God, Justin! He was so handsome! He was wearing a dark suit with a white shirt underneath. It's not what he was wearing when he died. Did I ever tell you how handsome he was?"

"I figured you would in time," I said.

She smiled, reached out, and grabbed my huge, red hand. She squeezed it, and I squeezed in return.

"He's tall," she said. "Well, not by *your* standards, but tall. Maybe six-four. I don't even come up to his chin. He has big, dark eyes, like Charlie's." I couldn't help but smile at this. "He was such a gentleman.

"I remember a few years ago when the kids were younger . . . I was having one of those days when they're just awful, when they're not listening to anything you say, just having a bad day, you know? Well, maybe you *don't* know, but . . . anyway, I was screaming at them, telling them to leave me alone, to go to their rooms for a few minutes, and give me some peace and quiet. They were acting so out of character, so . . . loud."

I couldn't picture Holly doing this, let alone the children misbehaving, not from what I'd seen.

"Carl came home early while I was trying to get supper ready. I was a nervous wreck. He took one look at me, and that was it. Carl always had a way of reading me. Maybe it wasn't hard because of the expression on my face. But he knew instantly. He wrapped his arms around me, giving me this great big hug, holding onto me for the longest time. I just cried and cried. I let go of him. I was afraid I was burning the pork chops, so I turned back to the stove. He came over and stood beside me, nudged me lightly with his hip, just enough to push me out of the way, and said, 'Move over, buster. I'm taking over this popcorn stand. Your job is to retire to the living room, have a glass of wine, and wait for me to call when dinner's ready. That's an order. Go on now, get!' I just stood there, crying. 'Go on, get moving,' he said, but I couldn't move. I just stood there crying, stressed out, and frazzled by the kids. I just bawled and bawled. I'm such a bawl baby. I cry at everything.

"Carl said, 'Hey, champ, I didn't mean to tell you what to *do*. It was just a suggestion to take a load off. Do you need another hug? Just let it out, Holly. Just let it out.' So, I did. He fixed us both a drink, took my hand, and pulled me into the living room. He sat me down. He went upstairs and was gone for about ten minutes, talking to the kids. Suddenly, the house was very quiet. He came back downstairs, finished making dinner, set the table, and we all sat down to eat. We had one of the best meals we'd ever had. We all laughed and talked. The kids behaved. I don't know what he said, but whatever it was, it worked. Whenever Carl was gone and I was left alone with them, they were more behaved, especially when he came home. I mean, kids will be kids, right? They'll tease each other, but knowing Carl was coming home, they were better . . . after school . . . during the summer. And when he *did* come home, things were different. We were the perfect family . . . until . . ." She stared out the window again.

"He sounds like quite a guy, Holly," I said. "I like him already, and I don't even know him. You were lucky to have him. And he was lucky to have you. You had beautiful children together. That must count for something, don't you think?"

She turned away from the window and looked at me. "He said . . ." she began and stopped for a second before going on. "He said that he'd always be here. No matter what. Not before he died, Justin. Just now . . . when I saw him. He told me you and Karen are very special people and that I should trust and listen to everything you say. He came right over to the bed. He sat right where you're sitting now. He grabbed my hand. I could smell his aftershave. I could feel the strength in his hands. I could feel how warm he was. God, Justin, it was so *real!* He leaned over and kissed me on the forehead. He told me it was important for me to be strong, stronger than ever because things were different now. Things were different and would always be different, but it wasn't over. Not even close. He told me I had to be strong for you and Karen . . . that I had to be strong for the kids. 'Be strong, most importantly, for *you,* Holly,' he said. 'Be strong for you.'"

She stopped and stared into space as if reliving the moment. I wonder if she could still smell him, feel the warmth of his hand, and surprisingly—whether I believed it or not—I could detect the slight aroma of aftershave.

Holly continued:

"'Promise me you'll be strong for yourself, Holly,' he told me. 'Promise me, no matter what, that you'll be strong for you.' I started crying again. I couldn't help it. 'I will, Papa,' I said. I sometimes called him Papa, because he loved Ernest Hemingway and always talked about how he wanted to go to Africa."

I had no idea what she was talking about because I had no idea what Africa was *or* Ernest Hemingway.

"'I promise,' I told him. 'I miss you so much.' He smiled at me. 'I know,' he said. 'I love and miss you, too, Holly. But I'm not really gone, and I need you to remember that. It's important. Okay?' I promised again. I couldn't stop crying. He patted my hand, stood, and went to the window. The next thing I knew, he was gone. He just disappeared. He turned to the window and walked right through it into that ball of light, and I just . . . I just . . ."

She couldn't go on. I could see she couldn't go on. I told her not to worry about it. I told her she didn't have to say anything else. She looked toward the window again. I did, too. The stars had a different meaning to me now. I wasn't sure what to believe or how to respond, but I knew better than to second guess what she'd told me.

Holly turned back to me. She looked concerned. "Justin," she said. "Do you think I'm going crazy?"

I smiled and patted her hand. "Hardly," I said. "I think you're the farthest thing from crazy I've ever met. I think you're probably the sanest person I know."

I tried to absorb all that had happened since the collision. I watched Holly closely. She wasn't crying now. She looked better. I was glad I'd come up to see her. I was glad I'd knocked, and I hoped she felt the same.

This was stranger than anything I'd ever experienced. I was still trying to wrap my head around it.

"Do you feel better?" I asked.

She nodded. "Yes. Thank you, Justin."

I pulled the covers under her chin as if Holly were one of my own. Surprising myself, I leaned over and kissed her forehead. It was cool. "Do you think you can sleep now?" I asked.

She nodded.

"Good," I said. "And Holly?"

"Yes?"

"I think, no matter what's going on, or what's happening, no matter how bad some stuff may seem, some very beautiful things are happening. I think it's important for us to remember that. All of us. We have some good things to look forward to, despite the changes."

She nodded. When she smiled, I could tell she was going to be all right.

I went to the door and opened it. I turned and looked at her, at the ball of light hovering outside the window.

"Justin?"

I raised my black eyebrows.

"Thank you," she said.

I nodded. "I love you, Holly. Get some rest. Okay?"

I walked out and closed the door behind me.

I didn't know why I said what I did. It was strange, the most amazing thing in the world, but the most natural, too.

As I made my way down the hall, I realized I was crying for reasons *I* didn't understand.

Since landing on Earth, I was shedding my first mortal tears.

———

I walked downstairs into the lighted living room and laid next to Karen. She stirred and moved.

"Where have you been?" she asked, in a sleepy voice. She reached out and put her hand on my thigh.

"Holly had a dream," I said.

"Nightmare?" she asked.

"Just the opposite, I think."

"Is she okay?"

"Yes," I said. "Go to sleep."

"You first," she said, nudging closer, and put her arm around my chest.

I stared at the ceiling, wide awake.

I held onto her and thought about Holly and the kids, Carl, Dilladale, Lane, and Tor-Latress, everything and anything in the world that would keep me awake for the rest of the night. I didn't care. Some of it was pleasant to think about. I thought about Charlie and his magic trick. I thought about Cerras lying asleep in a frozen cave. I thought about the community coming together earlier and the surprising compassion I'd witnessed.

Sleep didn't claim me for a long, long time.

4.

Flowers for Carl and a Belated Gift

The next day, Karen had the children enthralled in the backyard with one of her many tales of Paramis and the Old Ones, reminding me of the day I'd met her. She'd been doing the same thing in Delayne when I happened to walk by. Her power to enchant had stopped me dead in my tracks.

But that's another story . . .

The search for Lane was still underway. According to the latest, she was gathering followers up north, mainly people from Earth. She'd convinced them we were the reason for the change, and they believed her. She planned on destroying us all, along with the Old Ones. People were flocking to her, including her own kind, which surprised me.

Meanwhile, we bided our time with Holly and the kids. I was in the kitchen with her, helping her make sandwiches for lunch. She seemed more her old self today, although her eyes were puffy from crying the night before. I looked at the sliding glass door leading to the backyard. It was a beautiful day. Clouds patched an intense blue sky. The grass was rich and green.

"Thank you for last night, Justin," Holly said.

I shrugged. "Hey, man, it was nothing," I said, adopting Charlie's vernacular.

She looked at me, raised her eyebrows, and I shrugged. Maybe I would leave that kind of talk for the kids.

"How long has Charlie been into magic?" I asked.

Holly smiled and looked outside at her boy. She was wearing a dark green sweater with buttons down the front, a white shirt underneath. Her hair was in a ponytail.

"A few years," she said. "We rented a documentary about magicians one night. It was David Copperfield he liked best. He was hooked from that moment on."

"David Copperfield?"

"A magician. Very popular. Not so much anymore. I remember I saw him on television when I was a kid. He made the Statue of Liberty disappear."

I could've kept asking questions all night about people, places, and things, so I stuck to the David Copperfield topic instead.

"Huh," I said, feeling uninformed. "Like an entertainer?"

Holly nodded. "Yes," she said. "Don't you have magicians on Paramis?"

I shrugged. "I guess. But they don't entertain. Magic on Paramis is used differently."

Holly nodded. "Carl and I were going to get him a top hat and cape for his birthday. "Of course, we didn't expect the collision."

"When was his birthday?"

"December second. Sometime during the collision. Funny, he always looked forward to his birthday. He didn't mention anything about it this year. Maybe because of Carl. I think Jody and Mellicent explained things to him, and he's handling it better because of that. He hasn't mentioned his father since that night." She paused. "I guess he *should* have a birthday. Seems kind of silly for him *not* to have one."

"What was the hat you mentioned?"

"Huh? Oh! A top hat. Uh. I don't have a picture. I'd have to draw one for you."

She found a pencil and a piece of paper, drawing a picture of what a top hat looked like.

"I'm not an artist," she said, turning the paper my way.

"Interesting," I said, storing the information in the back of my mind.

We finished making sandwiches. Holly opened the back door, calling the kids in for lunch. We sat around the table in the dining room, Charlie beating his legs against the legs of his chair. Karen continued to tell tales of our world.

Here we were, the rarest of families, the weirdest of all, tall, strangely-colored dragons with Holly and her kids, as if it were the most natural thing in the world.

Charlie bobbed his head back and forth to some tune only he could hear. We smiled at him. We sat laughing and talking until the oddness of the situation nailed me. More and more, the longer we were there, the weirder the situation became. No matter how odd it was, I couldn't help feeling entranced by Holly and her kids. Something was magical about them in ways that surpassed the magic on Paramis.

The collision had done things I couldn't put a label to.

—

After lunch, Holly took Charlie into the living room and had a private conversation with him. I assumed it was about Carl's death. I think Charlie already knew about Carl and understood his father was gone, but I think Holly talked to him more for her sake than for Charlie's.

In the kitchen, I looked at Jody and Mellicent. "You girls, okay?" I asked.

"Sure," Jody said. They were pretty girls with dark brown hair like their mother.

Mellicent nodded. "But what happens to us now?" she said. "I mean, not just with Dad gone, but since everything's so different?"

I looked at Karen. Her eyes were wide. I figured I should be as honest with them as I could. "I really don't know," I said. "There's so much happening, so much to sort out. We're still waiting for word from Dilla-dale."

They didn't say anything. Jody and Mellicent were mysterious girls as if harboring some deep, inner wisdom.

Holly and Charlie came back into the kitchen. Charlie seemed troubled. I wonder if he understood the concept of death.

"We should probably say goodbye to him," Holly said. "It's been long enough, I think."

"We'll wait for you," I said.

"No," Holly said adamantly. "In fact, Justin, I would like it very much if you came with us."

I looked at Karen, who simply shrugged.

"Are you sure?" I asked.

Holly nodded. "We'll get him some flowers," she said. "I think we all need to say goodbye to him in our own way, especially the kids."

"Here's some flowers, Mom," Charlie said, holding a bouquet of brightly colored flowers in his hand.

None of us saw him do the trick. He—as he'd done the night before—simply plucked them from mid-air.

We all looked at each other and smiled.

"You're going to have to get some new tricks before that one gets stale," Mellicent said.

"Yeah," Charlie said. "But it's so *cool.*"

Holly burst out laughing. So did the girls. Eventually, Karen and I laughed along with them, but Charlie just looked confused.

"What's so funny?" he asked.

———

We walked out of the house and down the road in the warm sunshine. It took us twenty minutes to get there. Karen and I lagged behind while Holly and the kids walked ahead of us. I watched them carefully.

"Do you see that?" I asked.

Karen gripped my hand. "I've been watching it for a while," she said. "I'm just not sure I understand it . . . let alone believe it."

I continued to watch Holly and her children. I wondered if they could see it in one another, a silvery golden light surrounding them in an umber-like mist. Holly turned and asked what was taking us so long. We quickened our pace and soon caught up with them.

I still couldn't get over the neighborhood, how the trees intertwined with stop signs, houses, cars, and telephone poles. I didn't mention the umber I'd seen, and neither did Karen.

Holly, carrying Charlie's flowers, walked ahead, holding his hand. They were all holding hands, a family chain connected at the palm. Watching this close-knit family was interesting in ways I couldn't describe.

Once at the house, Karen and I hung back. One by one, Holly and her children dropped to their knees and bowed their heads. I wondered what kind of god they were praying to.

When they were done, Holly set the flowers down where the front porch angled upward, facing the sky. Birds filled the trees in a strangely warped and rolling yard.

After a time, they stood up. Holly looked to where she'd placed the flowers. She turned and embraced each of her kids, kissing them on the cheek. Holly was smiling; there was something different about her. She looked more at peace, untroubled. It was a relief to see.

They walked toward us. Jody said, very softly, "Bye, Daddy." She turned and waved at the house. Her eyes were glossy with tears. When I caught a glimpse of her, she quickly looked away.

Holly sighed, putting her hand on my arm. "Thank you," she said.

"You keep saying that, Holly, but it's not necessary," I said.

"Yes, it is," she said. She turned to the children. "Come on, kids. Let's figure out what we're gonna have for dinner. There's gotta be something to eat besides sandwiches all the time."

"*A-men,*" Mellicent said, dramatically.

They walked ahead of us. Something strange was happening to me lately, and I wanted to know what it was—think about it for a while. Something was going on, some semblance of understanding. If I concentrated hard enough, I'd be able to grasp it. Things were moving too quickly, though. I had a hard time keeping up. I wasn't sure what was going on, no more than the rest of them, but the Underhills had me under their spell. They were teaching me something. Whatever it was, was vital. I just didn't know what that thing was.

I looked at Karen, and she smiled at me. I looked behind me, toward the house. For a minute, I thought a vandal, a thief, had come to steal the flowers.

A man was standing near the porch, holding the flowers to his face. I thought of the night before, of Holly's description: Carl Underhill. He wore a black sport-coat, a white shirt underneath as Holly had described. His hair was almost black, styled thick and wavy, combed back from a high forehead. His skin was slightly tanned, not the pale hue of a ghost. He picked up the flowers and held them to his face, inhaling their fragrance. He smiled and nodded to himself, as if thinking of something only he knew about, reliving a memory of his family, perhaps.

Was I imagining this? Could it be real? Was I, for the first time, looking at an actual ghost?

I stopped. Karen stopped as well. She followed my gaze. Her surprise mirrored my own. A gasp escaped her throat. I was looking at something impossible, a miracle, but it wasn't.

It was real.

Carl looked up as if sensing our presence and met our eyes. He smiled, nodded to both of us, and his eyes seemed to brighten. He put his hand in the air and waved at us. I felt silly, but I couldn't help raising my own hand in return.

He nodded a single time, still smiling, and turned. He didn't put the flowers back but took them with him. He turned his head toward the sky, then lowered it to take another whiff of the flowers.

I was dumbstruck. I opened my mouth to say something, but nothing came out. I felt paralyzed. I couldn't get over how puzzling and incredible this was. Something stirred in my breast, an alien feeling I'd never felt before.

A magical world, I thought? Sure, Paramis was magical, but what about the world we were in? How could I explain it? My understanding of this planet was insignificant compared to its wonders. There was more going on here than I could comprehend. Even if Cerras explained it to me, I wouldn't be able to grasp it.

I shook my head and turned. Still holding Karen's hand, we hurried to catch up to Holly and her kids.

—

When we got back, I turned to Karen. No one was as somber as I'd thought, but they were quieter than usual.

"I want to go into town," I told Karen. "Wanna come with me?"

"What are you going into town for?" she asked.

"It's a surprise."

She raised her thick, black eyebrows. We told Holly we'd be back later. She gave us a puzzled expression. Not to worry, I told her in a glance. It would be worth it.

We left the house, transforming into dragons for the first time since we'd arrived on Earth. We took to the sky. The shift came, and with it, a sense of peace. It felt good to be flying again, the cool wind against my wings. I realized we had yet to show Holly and the kids our 'other' forms. At the rally, they'd seen glimpses of it, but not the whole thing.

I closed my eyes, the brisk wind against my scales. Below, Paramis Altered and New Earth unfolded under us. I flapped my wings slowly and savored the view.

Changing into dragons is more a focused, centralized thought. Massive wings spread wide, and we are—in all aspects—similar to many pictures your Earth artists convey. Of course, when we're dragons, we can't talk, but we issue a loud, echoing cry and breathe a blistering cloud of fire.

I didn't know what to look for at first. I was going on instinct. The department store might have what I was looking for, but after our visit, I couldn't remember seeing anything like what I was looking for now. Karen was persistent, wanting to know what the mystery was. I could've made it easier by asking Holly *where* to look, but I wanted it to be a surprise for her as well.

We found a shopping mall several miles away in another town. The collision had swallowed most of it, making the entrances inaccessible. Finally, I took to a larger town, one I didn't know the name of, at the base of large, red-colored rocks.

We transformed again, taking to the streets. Karen pointed to a store I hadn't noticed.

"Is *that* what you're looking for?" she asked.

I followed where she pointed, a store called All Occasion Costumes and grabbed her hand. I didn't know how she knew.

We walked across the street. The shop was open, still intact. Some places, like Holly's newer house, were untouched by the collision. The costume shop was one of them. I walked inside. The silence was eerie. The shop was deserted. Lines of costumes, masks, display cases of makeup took up the entire store. I walked through, staring at goblin masks, alien heads, a skull with a forked tongue between dry, green teeth. What kind of festivals did these people celebrate, I wondered?

"They like their entertainment, don't they?" I asked Karen.

She smiled at me, looking at a long white robe. It made me think of Dilla-dale.

Behind the counter on a shelf high up on the wall was the thing I was looking for. I reached up and took it down. It might be a little big for Charlie, but remembering Holly's drawing, I knew this was a top hat. It was beautiful, black silk, absolutely perfect. The price on the tag said $120.00. I didn't have any money. I felt awkward for a minute, thinking of Granger's speech . . . the thievery and looting. I still felt guilty for our ransacking of the department store and wondered if I should turn myself in.

As I turned, holding it up for Karen, she must've read my mind again. She was holding up a black cape with red silk lining underneath.

"It might be a little big," I said, looking at the hat. "But he can always grow into it." I walked around the counter and put the hat on Karen's head. "It's you," I said.

"It's too small," she said, taking it off.

I leaned over and kissed her. "I don't know," I said. "Maybe we could create a new fashion trend."

"Dragons are not made for hats," she said.

"Depends on the dragon," I said.

Her powder blue skin turned pink, and she looked down.

"Karen," I said. "I haven't seen you blush in quite a while."

"Come on," she said, rolling her eyes. "sometimes you can be rather insufferable."

We left the store. No one would miss the costume, so I didn't feel too guilty about taking it.

We took to the sky and flew back to Holly's house, changing back once more before we hit the ground. The dark was coming on, the light in the west fading over the mountains. The stars shifted, moving here and there, lighting the neighborhood.

I walked into Holly's house with Karen behind me. She was holding the cape and the hat behind her back.

"Hi," Holly said. "You weren't gone very long." She wore a burgundy and blue sweater with a strange looking A on the front, a sweeping trail of snow. It looked like an emblem, but I couldn't make out what it meant.

"Where's Charlie?" I asked.

"Up in his room," she said. "Why?"

"We have a surprise for him," Karen told her.

"You might want to get everyone together," I said. "We got him a late birthday present."

"I wished I'd have known," Holly said. "I could've baked a cake. I think the electricity is being more consistent."

Holly went upstairs to get the kids. One by one, they trotted down.

"What's the gig?" Mellicent said.

"We heard Charlie missed his birthday," Karen said. "So we got him a present."

61

"Hopefully, it's stilts to make him taller," Jody said. She and Mellicent burst out laughing.

"Heard you had a birthday a while back, Charlie," I said. "Sorry, we didn't have time to wrap it."

He looked curious but didn't say anything.

"Do you mind if we give you a late birthday present?" Karen asked.

Charlie shrugged as if it didn't matter to him one way or the other. "Sure," he said.

"This is from all of us, Charlie," Karen said. "We all saved up our gold and silver coins and chipped in. Hope you like it."

She pulled her hands out from behind her back, bringing the top hat and cape into view. Charlie's eyes lit up. He beamed, smiling from ear to ear. Holly was also smiling, along with Jody and Mellicent.

"That's pretty cool," Mellicent said, trying to downplay it.

"Wow!" Charlie said, stepping forward. "That is *tight!"*

"Actually," I said, not understanding his jargon. "It might be a little big."

Everyone laughed for reasons I didn't understand. I blushed stupidly.

"Boys shouldn't miss their birthdays," I said. "Your mom told me. I hope it's okay."

I said this more for the kids' approval than anyone else's. Holly sensed it and nodded. I was glad we decided to get the hat and cape.

"Can I try them on?" Charlie said, excitedly, turning to his mom, who shrugged.

"I'd be a witch if I told you no," she said.

Karen handed Charlie his new outfit. He put the hat on. It was somewhat large, but it only added to his charm. He put on the cape, clasping the hook together in front of his neck. He moved in a quick circle, making the cape twirl. We all laughed and clapped.

"Do a trick, Charlie," Jody said.

"Yeah, Charlie," Mellicent said. "No more flowers. Let's see what you can *really* do."

Charlie looked at each of us. He pushed the brim up out of his eyes. Despite being slightly big, the outfit looked perfect.

"And now!" he said, theatrically. "Ladies and gentlemen! I will perform a feat to dazzle the senses! You won't believe your eyes!

Watch closely now while the Great Charlie is here one minute and gone the next . . . Abracadabra!"

I was smiling as wide as he was, entranced.

He wrapped the cape around himself, covering his face. Before it unfurled, he vanished completely.

—

Ten seconds later, he came walking down the stairs, still wearing the hat and cape. We all clapped and cheered.

"Bravo!" we cried.

Near the bottom of the stairs, Charlie took off the hat and bowed. He was blushing but enjoying himself at the same time.

"Thank you," he said, bowing again. "You've been a *great* audience!"

—

The next day was bright and cloudless with a brisk breeze in the morning air. The neighborhood had settled down, and things were returning to normal again—as much as they were able to. We still hadn't heard anything from Dilla-dale or the others, and I was starting to feel useless.

After breakfast, Charlie asked:

"So, if you're really dragons, how come you don't *look* like dragons?"

I'd been waiting for this. Charlie was still wearing his hat and cape. I figured he wasn't going to take them off anytime soon. He probably slept in them.

"Would you like us to *prove* that we're dragons?" I asked.

He grinned. Jody's and Mellicent's eyes grew wide.

"Let's go outside," I said. "There's more room out there."

The family followed. Holly looked intrigued and worried at the same time. I assumed she was concerned with how we might terrify the children, but I told her there was nothing to be afraid of. Karen and I stood on the front lawn. I looked over at her, and she shrugged, as if telling me to go first. I nodded and willed the shift. For a second, a slight humming sound filled my ears, then a flash of red.

I was as big as one of the smaller moving vans I'd seen. We're not enormously grotesque dragons, but we *do* grow in size with the change. I could carry all three of Holly's children on my back without any effort. I looked at the kids, then at Holly. Their eyeballs were enormous, perhaps a trifle fearful.

Karen changed after me, a resplendent, beautiful blue dragon with big, black eyes and powder blue scales. Our hair was gone. I spread my massive wings and took to the sky, letting out a loud cry. I noticed several people on their lawns watching in amusement, including a woman across the street who was planting flowers.

I flew up to the top of the house and hooked my talons into the shingles. I kept my wings spread, angled my head toward the sky, and roared. A great, rolling ball of fire billowed from my mouth and disappeared in a plume of smoke.

Karen flew as high as she dared, then plummeted fast to the ground. Before she hit the grass, she willed the change and was Karen again. I flew down from the roof and landed beside her, willing the change back, and looked at Karen.

"Show off," she said.

"Holy cow! Holy jeez!" Charlie exclaimed. His eyes were enormous. *"That was the coolest thing I've ever seen! Did you guys see that? Holy cow! Holy jeez!"*

Holly, Jody, and Mellicent looked at us with wide eyes, but they didn't seem as thrilled. They looked more shocked than anything, or perhaps awed was a better word. It was hard to tell.

"We didn't scare you, did we?" I asked Holly.

She was quick to shake her head. "No," she said. "I . . . you're . . . beautiful," she finished.

Jody and Mellicent nodded.

I raised my sinister eyebrows. "Beautiful?" I asked as if the very thought were absurd.

She nodded.

"I don't think I've ever been called that before," I said.

"I think they were talking about *me,* sweetheart."

Karen had adopted their sarcastic sense of humor, and she was using it now on a regular basis.

5.
Karen

Dearest Justin,

I don't know if you remember the time we met. I guess I'd be upset with you if you didn't. I've wanted to write to you for a long time, and this might be a letter a long time coming. Sometimes, it's hard to tell you how I feel exactly, and this is the only way I can express it. I know what you're about to say, so just keep it to yourself, lover boy. I'm here to remind you how important we are for each other, so just get used to it. And don't make a bunch of gagging noises, please. I'm trying to be sincere.

Gill says he likes you a lot, and Gill is skeptical of most dragons, especially the red ones. The first time he saw you, you were leaning against a thatched cottage in the middle of Delayne. You were smiling from ear to ear, he says. I was fabricating one of the many stories I tell about Paramis, the Old Ones, and Cerras. I don't remember the tale exactly. I have to keep my audience mesmerized, and there are a lot of children on Paramis, as you well know. I had a group of maybe forty kids around me. I was sitting on a small stool, while Gill, being the joker and thespian he is, acted out the tales according to how I told them, landing on his hands when I told a joke, or mimicking a sword fight between men, or flying when the situation called for it. Gill is always a good sport, and the children laugh and love his antics.

He approached me later after I told the story, and the kids returned to their homes. "I believe, dear Karen," he told me, folding his purple arms across his chest, "that you have an admirer."

I raised my eyebrows. "Who, pray tell, would that be?"

"Did you not see the red dragon by the cottage?" he asked.

"I can't say I did."

"Well, I saw the red dragon," Gill said, adding drama to his description. "And he is a dragon to watch out for. He breathes a scalding, yet freezing cloud of flame. His skin is the hue of smoldering coals, his eyes as red as rubies. I have seen this

monstrosity in the clouds and have challenged him once to a fight. He laughed, declining my offer, saying he didn't want to humiliate me in the eyes of the Old Ones. Rather arrogant, that. Though, I don't believe he is an evil dragon. He is a superior beast, schooled by the Old Ones, if not a trifle cocky."

I shook my head because when he gets in this mood, there's nothing you can do. Any game you play only fuels his fire.

"Gill," I said. "Your drama is poorly played."

He raised his eyebrows at me. "Oh?" he said. "Perhaps you'd care to be informed that he has appeared day after day in the same square, in the middle of town, listening to you weave your enchantments to the children. I have seen him, sister of mine, and he has a huge smile on his face day in and day out. And there is only one purpose behind a smile like that. Trust me, I know. So, call it what you will. He's an admirer. I believe—if I may be so bold—that our red fire-dragon fancies you."

You know how Gill is, Justin. He's the sweetest brother a girl could have, if not a little obnoxious.

I thought nothing of it at the time, but he was persistent.

"See, tomorrow," he said. "Look, when you are telling your tales to the children, and you'll find him. He'll be there."

Of course, the very next day, as I told my tales, I looked for you. And, of course, Gill was playing with me again because you were nowhere to be found. You were, in fact, nowhere at all, as if you'd read Gill's mind and decided to play a game yourself, which I'd learned later was exactly what you did. You are quite the nefarious dragon when you put your mind to it, Justin. I think it's the reason you have the color skin you do.

I was finishing one of my stories, and the children were drawn to Gill as he blew fire from his mouth, enthralling them with juggling, walking on his hands, and transforming as only he can do. Gill is a thespian, but I have to admit, he is strangely loveable when it comes to the younger ones. They do adore him immensely.

And, of course, you startled me.

"You have quite the natural ability."

My heart leaped into my throat. I turned, and there you were, a blazing inferno of a dragon, smiling at me.

"Sneaking up on ladies is not a way to win their affections," I said.

"Forgive me, milady," you said. "But I couldn't help it. For the last week, I've watched you enthrall the children of Delayne. I admit I've found myself under the same hypnotic spell. You have witchcraft in your voice, Karen."

"How did you know my name?"

"Your brother, Gill, told me," you said. "I accosted him earlier and asked if any suitor had claimed your powder blue hand. He politely told me no. I asked him if I had his blessing, and he laughed and told me, of course. I like your brother. He's a gentleman, very talented."

I looked over at Gill, who, of course, noticed we were talking. I shot him a deadly glare, and all he did was hold his palms up.

"I already have a suitor," I said. "And he is not a dragon of conceited conflagration like you."

"You wound my heart, my dear," you said. "And you lie."

"I'm not interested in a suitor," I said, looking away, "and I'm perfectly happy on my own."

You smiled because you knew I was lying as well. All of us dragons and our different talents!

The fact is, Justin, you mesmerized me. I'll be honest. And I think what drew me to you was the fact that you were drawn to my stories, the fact that I enchant the children with ancient tales of gods and the Old Ones. I do love the children, and I knew you understood this. And I think you were enchanted by them as well. It explains so much about you, despite your nefarious appearance.

That's why I couldn't say no.

That was many years ago, of course. You and Gill became good friends, and we all shared the wisdom we'd learned from the Old Ones. I think that wisdom is what brought us closer together.

For more than seventy years, I've been with you now. I don't regret a single minute.

I have a feeling there's a change in the air, however, and I'm not sure what that means, but I know it's coming soon. I don't know if I'll ever give you this letter, but I want you to know (as I write this in the library of Delayne) that in my own silly way, you mean the world to me. You treat me with fairness and equality, and I think we learn a lot from each other.

I look forward to many years with you still, and I hope the future spans a lifetime of happiness, my dear dragon.

For the moment, I'm going to close this letter. I have a feeling there will be many more in the future. Sometimes, it's just the best way for me to express myself. Maybe someday, when we are old dragons and sitting around the ancient tables of the Old Ones, I'll read them to you if you'll let me.

Thank you for your patient kindness and your gentle heart, despite your wicked guise. I know, deep down, better than anyone, that you're the farthest thing from wicked.

Thank you for being with me, for the love you share, and for your strength and courage.

Always yours, forever . . .
Karen.

6.
Charlie

School wasn't all that great to begin with. I had some friends I liked there, and they thought it was cool I did card tricks and all, seeing their eyes get big and stuff. I would do some things at home for Mom and Dad, but nothing like what I've done lately. Dad was always cool about my magic tricks. He'd get the family together and say things like: "Gather round everybody! The Great Charlie is about to dazzle our eyes with impossible feats! Gather round, gather round!"

Dad was always doing stuff like that. He liked the performances more than I did. He was my assistant. He'd tie me up, and I'd slip through the ropes without any effort at all. Once, he tied me up pretty good, and I *couldn't* get out. I forgot a crucial part of the trick, but I can't tell you what it was because it's a secret, and magicians never tell.

I looked at Dad and said, "Another trick?"

"Huh?" he asked.

Mom, Jody, and Mell were sitting on the couch. They raised their eyebrows.

"I can't get out," I told Dad.

"You can't get *out?"* he said, looking confused.

Mom and my sisters looked at one another. Jody started laughing.

"I pooped it, Pop," I said. "I shanghaied the booby-shoot. I plucked the peacock's feathers."

Mell started giggling. She knew this was my form of swearing. Everyone else just looked at me like I was crazy.

I was tied to one of the dining room chairs. My feet were tied to the legs. (That sounds funny, doesn't it?) My hands were tied behind me. I couldn't feel my hands because they were so numb from the ropes.

"You mean, you screwed the pooch?" Dad said.

"Carl!" Mom said from the couch, blushing. Boy, was her face red!

Jody and Mell burst out laughing again. I didn't know what was so funny. I still couldn't feel my hands and feet, and my ears were getting tingly.

"Yes, Dad," I said. "Pooch screwed."

"*Charlie!*" Mom said, and that made everyone laugh again.

Dad just stood there as if he couldn't believe it. "But you're the Great *Charlie!*" he said as if that explained everything. "I might add, in fact, that you are the *greatest* magician the state of Colorado has ever seen, and there's no doubt in my mind, Son, that you can get out of *any* knot!"

"Not this one," I told him. "Jeez, Dad, I'm only nine. I'm just starting to get the hang of this stuff!"

Dad looked like I'd broken his heart. "But how's that possible?" he said. "I don't understand it."

"Come on, Dad, untie them," I said. "I don't have any feeling in my hands and feet."

Jody and Mell kept laughing. We settled for simple card tricks instead. Although I think they were disappointed, they were still entertained.

I miss those days, and I miss Dad, too.

Despite all that, I couldn't get the dreams out of my head. I'd had weird dreams lately . . . lots of them. I didn't think too much about them at first, not until I started having them all the time. I thought they were just nightmares. But there was something nice about them, too. It was weird, as if I were looking through the eyes of another world, and it was filled with more magic than I'd ever dreamed of!

A shape hovered outside my bedroom window. It came night after night, hovering there like a huge bat. Or the figure of a man, only it had huge, black wings. Sometimes, I got the impression it wasn't a dream at all. Sometimes, you have dreams like that, when you wake up and you can't believe how real it is because you can taste and touch and smell things, and the colors are so vivid and everything.

Anyway, there was this thing outside my window, this creature made of shadow; only it wasn't a shadow. It was different. You could touch it. I know that sounds stupid, but it's true. It was . . . *alive*. It had thoughts, could talk, but I couldn't see its face. It had no eyes or mouth, just the form of a man with huge, shadowy bat-like wings; only he didn't have any legs, either.

There was a woman with him. She had different colored skin, but she was pretty. Her skin was solid green, like grass, and she had long red/orange hair, like fire, and yellow eyes. She carried a long sword at her waist.

She stood in my room while the bat-like creature hovered outside the window.

"Hello, Charlie," she said and smiled. Her voice was quiet, soft, and she sat on the edge of my bed. "Do you want to come outside with me? I want to show you something."

I shook my head, not so much at her, but at the thing outside the window.

"What's the matter?" the woman asked, frowning.

"There's something out there," I said. I was afraid, so I pointed to the window.

This was weird, I thought, because it was like I was dreaming, but like I was awake, too, like I'd just woken up. I was still in bed, but I wasn't sleeping. Was I awake now? But that couldn't be because there's no such thing as green-skinned women and shadowy monsters. At least I didn't think so.

The woman smiled and turned to the figure at the window.

"Go away, Latress," she said.

For a second, nothing happened. The shadowy thing got angry because it let out a strange cry. The next thing I knew, it was gone, like vanishing smoke.

"He can't hurt you, Charlie," the woman said. "Will you come outside with me now?"

I nodded and got out of bed. I walked downstairs and outside with the woman. It was different outside. It wasn't my neighborhood at all. I knew I had to be dreaming and that this wasn't real because the world was different. Ours was the only house on the block. There were no streets or roads. It was like being in the countryside. Dark mountains stood in front of us, lots of trees, a place I'd never seen or been before. The woman was tall, taller than Dad, and I felt really small next to her.

"What's your name?" I asked.

"Lane," she said. "I'm from Paramis, Charlie. That's where we are now."

"What's Paramis?"

"A world . . . much different than your own. Come on. Take my hand. I want to show you something."

I reached out and took her hand. I didn't think she was scary, except for maybe her yellow eyes. They were kinda spooky. But she was pretty, and she was nice to me, so I took her hand. When I did, the world changed again. We were in a place made of ice, and it was very cold. The wind was blowing. A million stars were in the sky, constellations I didn't recognize.

"Do you believe in gods, Charlie?" the woman asked.

"You mean, God?" I said.

"There is no *one* God, Charlie," she said. "Don't make that mistake. There are *many* gods. Some evil. Some good. We're going to see Cerras."

"Cerras?"

Lane nodded.

"There's an overall good, Charlie. But Cerras isn't part of it. He's evil, and we have to destroy him."

I was scared. I didn't want to see an evil god, but I wasn't sure how to get back home by myself, so I stayed with Lane.

"Don't worry, Charlie. He's already dead."

"Dead?"

Lane nodded again. "Harmless," she said. "Dead. He can't hurt us."

"Then why are we going to see him?"

"Because he's still powerful even *though* he's dead. His eyes are made of stars. There's great power in the Eyes of Cerras."

"But it's an *evil* power?" I asked.

"It *is* an evil power," Lane said. "But you and I are going to change all that."

She looked down at me and smiled. She gripped my hand tighter like she was trying to tell me everything was going to be all right. I didn't understand what she was talking about, so I nodded and followed her as we walked.

There were trees, but they were frozen. I didn't know how there could be frozen trees or how they could live, but I didn't say anything.

We came to a rocky canyon and entered a large icy cave. It was dark inside, and I couldn't see anything. I didn't want to go in there because it scared me.

"I can't see anything," I said.

"I can see well enough for both of us," Lane said.

Her voice sounded weird in the cave, hollow. I didn't want to let go of her hand in case I got lost. We walked for a long time. It seemed like forever. I slipped and almost fell several times because the path was uneven and frozen. Lane kept a hold of my hand and didn't let go.

After a while, I noticed a light up ahead, a yellow light, like Lane's eyes. I could see how big the cave was now. It smelled funny, too, and it was cold, but at least it was out of the wind. The walls of the cave shimmered with bright red and blue crystals, like rubies and sapphires. When we came to the yellow light, I saw it was a giant person lying on his back. He was huge, the size of a football field. He was made of gems, diamonds, and crystals of all kinds. The light was shining in all directions off his body and off the cave walls.

"That's Cerras," Lane whispered, as if afraid to wake him up.

Silver lights, blue lights, red lights, green, yellow, and orange. I wondered how something so beautiful could be evil. It didn't feel evil to me. It was the most beautiful thing I'd ever seen.

I looked at Lane. She didn't look at me. I saw the reflection of light swirling through her yellow eyes.

Then I *was* scared because the shadowy thing outside my window was there again. I felt it at the back of my head, at my neck, moving around me like smoke. I couldn't see very well.

The light in the cave from Cerras wasn't as bright suddenly. Black spots moved in front of my eyes. I was blinded. I couldn't see Lane or Cerras, only the black thing that was Latress.

"You're magical, Charlie," Lane said, kneeling down and whispering in my ear. "Do you realize that? You're very magical, and I need your help."

I was losing my balance. Wavering, like Dad sometimes gets at Christmas when he makes those drinks. He calls them, Caca-cola. Not for little boys. I don't know why he'd want to drink something called, Caca-cola, but maybe it's a Christmas thing.

"I want you to lift out the Eye of Cerras for me, Charlie," Lane said.

Latress was gone. Just like that. I could see everything in the cave again, the shimmering giant made of colored diamonds.

"Climb up onto his face and lift out his Eye. You can do that, okay? Cerras won't feel a thing."

That seemed like a stupid thing to do. Lift out his Eye? Wouldn't that blind him, make him wake up? *I* would wake up if someone tried to pluck out one of *my* eyes.

"Lift out his Eye, Charlie. And I'll give you something special, okay? Anything you want. You just tell me what it is. All you have to do is lift out his Eye."

I didn't care about anything like that. I didn't want to lift out Cerras' Eye. I didn't think he was really dead. If he was dead, why was he shining so brightly? Wouldn't the lights be out? What if he woke up and found me sitting on his face? What if he squashed me like a bug?

Besides, I thought Cerras was beautiful, the most beautiful thing I'd ever seen, and I didn't want to hurt him.

"Don't be scared, Charlie," Lane said. "Cerras is dead, remember? He won't miss it. He won't bite."

"I don't want to," I said.

Lane sighed. I was making her mad. She turned me around and put her hands on my shoulders. I couldn't believe how beautiful she was.

"Charlie," she said. "I have to tell you this, okay? So, listen carefully. Worlds are going to be destroyed. Your world and my world, both. This is not supposed to happen. People are going to die. Millions and millions of people. People from *two* worlds. Your mom and dad, your sisters. My kin, my brethren. This is the only way you can prevent that from happening. The Eyes of Cerras are very powerful, especially when used for good. Only they're really stars. They can put things right again, but no one can do it from our world, Charlie. Only *you* can. You'll be saving lives. You'll be saving two worlds at the same time and all of those lives. You'll be a hero. Do you understand that? I can't do it by myself because I'm not magical like you are. But *you* can. You can because you *are* magical and because you own more magic than both worlds combined. Do you understand that? Those card tricks, those things you do, are just illusions. There's something deeper inside you, Charlie. You'll be tapping into that magic now, and the Eye of Cerras will make you more magical than you can imagine. You'll be saving millions and millions of lives."

I looked at the massive Sleeping God and nodded. If it were to save lives, then I would do it. I didn't care about being a hero or anything like that, but I didn't want anyone to get hurt, either.

"Okay," I said, and Lane took a deep breath.

She stood up and looked at Cerras. "Good boy," she said.

I walked over to the sleeping giant, the dead giant, whatever he was. His huge arm lay alongside his body. I walked over, grabbing hold of the shimmering diamonds, and climbed up onto his stomach. The diamonds were very sharp, and I had to be careful grabbing them. One cut my palm, but I didn't want to cry in case it made Lane angry.

I stood up and walked slowly across his chest. I climbed up onto his chin, to Cerras' nose. I stopped at his huge eyeball. It was already open. His eyes weren't closed. I thought he must be awake. I remembered Mom telling me once that some people can sleep with their eyes open. Jody does that sometimes, which is kinda creepy, and I thought that's what Cerras was doing.

All of a sudden, I was wearing a magician's cape and a top hat. I knew it must be a dream because that kind of stuff doesn't happen in real life. And if this *was* a dream, what difference did it make? I would wake up. Everything would go back to normal, and I could just do this crazy thing, and Lane would leave me alone.

I looked into Cerras' Eye. It glowed with a silvery red light, a huge red diamond. I bent down and put my hands on each side of it. A loud hum moved through my body. It filled my ears. My head started to hurt, like bad music was playing loudly. Something happened when I touched it. I changed. I felt something change inside of me, making *me* different, but I didn't know what it was.

The Eye lifted out easily. It was only a piece of the Eye, not the whole thing, the colored pupil, like a massive gem. It was heavy but not heavy enough I couldn't carry it. It was as if the power of the Eye *helped* me lift it out, made it lighter for me to carry. It was so bright, my skin changed the same reddish, silvery color.

Suddenly, lights were bouncing everywhere off the cave walls. I closed my eyes because it hurt to look at, like diamonds on fire. I held the Eye in front of me and turned my face away.

After a while, it darkened. I opened my eyes again. I climbed off Cerras, holding the Eye. I was afraid I might stumble and drop it, shatter it in a million pieces. When I made it all the way off Cerras, I walked over to Lane and handed it to her. She took it but seemed scared for a minute like it was going to bite her. I told her it was okay to carry it, that it wouldn't harm her now that I'd removed it.

I heard something laugh inside my head. Then I heard the laughter all around. It was Latress.

Lane took the Eye and smiled. Her eyes were glowing.

Then I saw it, a shadowy specter, the slight outline of a man's face whispering into Lane's ear as she held the Eye of Cerras. An evil feeling was in the air again, as if the shadows were growing, expanding. It turned toward me. For a second, I could see its face. Two red eyes stared into mine. I could feel its hatred. I could feel its evil. It scared me, hissed at me, and I went cold all over. I wonder what I'd done, but suddenly the figure disappeared. It was just Lane and me in the cave again.

The ground started to tremble like an earthquake. The cave walls shook. Cerras began to shine again with a golden light.

"You did well, Charlie," Lane said. But there was something in her eyes I didn't like. It scared me. "You did very well."

From what I remembered, I was different; everything was different, but at least Lane and her shadow would leave me alone. At least they were gone.

I came out of a daze, but I wasn't sleeping in bed. It was like Lane had somehow stolen my body without my realizing it.

I was walking down the road with Mom, Mell, and Jody. Dad was home making a surprise dessert.

That's when the world went dark. That's when everything changed, and the dragons came.

There was something different about me. I could feel it inside. I could feel it in my body and in my head.

The magic I used to perform wasn't an illusion anymore.

It was real.

7.

Cerras

Cerras walked in silence, surveying the land. Across time and space, he'd come into existence by the Ones before him—the light of stars, shaped by forces beyond life and death to walk now among his creation. He'd given birth to Paramis and many worlds.

He'd created men, women, and Old Ones. He'd forged dragons from fire. They were protectors, sentient beings like the Old Ones, battling darkness and evil. The law of Cerras had been written on their hearts, and dragons had been borne to keep the law.

Cerras loved the land and those he gave life to. He loved the trees, mountains, rivers, and oceans. He walked under the stars in the stillness of the night and looked with joy upon all he'd made.

But he wanted to sleep. He wanted to bring worlds together, mixing the old with the new. There would be losses. Sacrifices would be made. There usually was for the greater good. And with it, there would be great gain. There would be catastrophe . . . because Cerras—though a god—was still bound by the laws of those who came before him.

There could be no light without darkness, no joy without sorrow, no love without pain. That was the pattern he wove throughout creation. History would be made while Cerras slept. He would witness it taking shape in his dreams.

But there was another . . . a brother born from age-old darkness, where the void of death and shadow thrived. Marrik was every inch Cerras' equal. His influence would spread wide in the minds of men and dragons, seeking power and dominion over all living things.

Cerras had an idea. If worlds could come together, if men and dragons could live in peace, then Light would reign. Heaven would descend to all worlds throughout the universe.

Because one thing conquered evil and darkness completely . . .
Unity.

8.
Pandemonium in the Land of Magma

After another week, we received word from Dilla-dale. A knock sounded at the door, and I got up to answer it. Dilla-dale looked as if he hadn't slept in a while. Dark circles sagged under his eyes. His hair was mussed. Granger and Preston were with him. Behind them stood Cullen, Lila, and Louis, like colorful dragon bodyguards. Charlie, Mellicent, and Jody were sitting on the couch with Holly. Karen stood just behind me.

"Any news?" Karen asked.

Dilla-dale looked pained. "Plenty of news," he said, stepping inside with the others. "None of it's good, I'm afraid."

"What's the matter?" I asked.

Dilla-dale looked at each of us in turn. The living room was small with all of us. "The factions are assembled up north. They're moving this way. I've never seen anything like it. Lane is moving her forces south, killing anyone and anything that stands in her way."

I looked at Karen. She looked at me.

"How is she able to move so swiftly?" Karen asked. "She couldn't have gotten that many people on her side already."

"Apparently, she has," Dilla-dale said. "Men and dragons, both. And she has the Eye of Cerras. She won't stop until she's killed everything in her path."

"This can't be happening," Karen said, looking alarmed.

"Villages, towns, houses." Dilla-dale shook his head. "Everything. It's all going up in flames. She's convinced everyone *we're* the reason the collision has happened, that we're trying to drive people off their own planet. She's turning dragons against men and men against dragons. Lane and Tor-Latress have used the Eye of Cerras to influence the minds of both. Her forces are moving this way. I came to warn you. We have to relocate . . . or . . ."

"Or what?" Karen asked.

"Or fight, I'm afraid," Dilla-dale said, not looking confident. "Tor-Latress guides her every move, but Lane is orchestrating the destruction. I think she has other help."

"Other help?" I asked.

"Marrik is awake. Cerras' twin."

Karen and I looked at each other again.

"I suggest we get moving, get the neighborhood relocated," Dilla-dale said. "It's going to be a mess, but we need people and dragons to help evacuate the neighborhoods in this area. We have some officials outside going door to door already."

"How much time do we have?" I asked.

"We have plenty of time for now," Dilla-dale said. "Granger and Preston have assembled their own forces. Do you know they have a military operation? It's quite astounding."

"We have guards and tanks, military equipment posted along the northern borders of town," Preston said. "We have front lines assembled, which should buy us some time. We have air strikes stationed and ready to go. But with the forces moving as fast as they are, these neighborhoods aren't safe."

"Where should we go?" I asked.

Granger shook his head, seemingly ashamed, as though all this were his fault.

"There's a community farther south about ten miles from here," Preston said. "It's been supplied already. We have buses coming in that can take the people there. We just have to get them ready."

"We'll do it," Karen said.

"We decided to put Dilla-dale in charge, and one called Murrochoe," Granger said.

"Murrochoe is here then?" I asked, turning to Dilla-dale.

Dilla-dale nodded. "He's helping, but he's old, Justin. He's a good counselor, but our main objective is the most dangerous one. We have to get the Eye and return it to Cerras."

"Won't that cause more destruction?"

Dilla-dale shrugged. "Not necessarily. Cerras is powerful, Justin. He's a god. No one can predict what his magic means, what his intentions are. But he's *our* god, and it's our duty to restore what is rightfully his. It's the law. The fate of both worlds may depend on it."

"As it is written on our hearts?" I asked.

"Yes," Dilla-dale said.

"I would like permission to relocate Holly and the kids personally," I said. "I would feel better about it."

"Of course. Get them someplace safe, but stick to the community to the south. You'll see the vehicles and the supplies. The battle is moving this way. After you're done, I want you and Karen with me. Lane has a plan of some kind. I think she's trying to absorb the power of the Eye, ingest it somehow, so it will destroy Cerras forever, which could, in turn, destroy the entire world."

"Doesn't she realize that?"

"She's mad, Justin."

I heaved a sigh.

"We'll get things moving right away," Karen said, nodding.

"Good," Dilla-dale said. "Meet us at the park where we held the meeting."

I nodded and looked at Holly. She and the kids looked frightened. She gathered them to her, putting her arms around them.

Dilla-dale said goodbye, and they left. Karen and I got some clothes, food, supplies, and prepared to relocate Holly and the kids.

I took a deep breath and steeled my heart against the future.

———

Cullen, Lila, and many from the local law enforcement helped organize the evacuation. The buses started rolling out. It felt selfish of me, but I felt Holly and the kids were my responsibility. I wanted to see them safely taken care of myself. Karen did, too.

Kids have a way of putting aside the chaos for new experiences, and they were doing so now. As we flew through the skies, Charlie, Mellicent, and Jody were laughing and having a good time. In my talons, I carried everything I could: food, clothes, and other belongings I thought they'd need. Charlie rode on my back with Mellicent. Jody and Holly rode on Karen. Under other circumstances, it might've been a pleasant flight, despite Charlie's laughter. I don't think he realized the extent of the danger we were in. If he did, he was choosing to handle it his own way. I thought about Carl and wondered what he'd think of his wife and kids flying over town on the backs of dragons.

I noticed the community soon enough, trucks and buses rolling in, pallets of supplies. There were plenty of homes here that had been evacuated after the collision. We found a small cabin for Holly and the kids near the foot of the mountains. Maybe the owners hadn't survived the collision. It was still furnished. Two bedrooms, two beds, one in each room, but I figured they could share, and it was only temporary.

We got Holly and the kids situated in their new home, close to the community in case they needed anything. After all the fun we'd had—the surprise with Charlie and his obvious magic—everything felt so serious and final. I could smell fire on the horizon and something else I didn't want to think about.

"Justin," Holly said, looking at me. There were tears in her eyes. "Please, be careful." She paused, looking frustrated, and bit her lower lip. "I wish there was something I could do. I feel so stupid and . . . helpless."

"The best thing you can do is stay here where it's safe," I said. "This will be over soon enough. We'll be back. I promise."

"Do you think we'll really be okay?" Mellicent said. She had tears in her eyes.

It was the first sign of doubt I'd seen from her. The gravity of the situation throttled me. These were just kids, but who was I to lie to them, to give them false hope?

Still, her emotion surprised me. I wanted to stay behind, to watch and protect them. The last thing I wanted was to face Lane. It wasn't cowardice. I cared more for the welfare of Holly and her children was all. I didn't want them out of my sight.

They were genuinely concerned, and they had every right to be. I understood. I wondered if we would ever see each other again and cursed myself for my lack of faith. What were the chances that Paramis and Earth could live side-by-side without war? I had my doubts, especially with Lane, and she had the Eye of Cerras.

"Of course, you'll be okay," I said, putting my hand on the back of Mellicent's head.

"Don't worry about anything, Holly," Karen said, her face stern. "We'll be back."

Holly looked doubtful. She stepped closer, embracing Karen. Karen hugged her in return. We all took turns . . . just in case, I suppose. I embraced Jody and Mellicent.

Charlie stepped toward me. "When it's all over," he said, as if the war were nothing more than a mere setback, "I want to ride on your back again. It's cold up there, but it was fun. I wish the kids at school could've seen it."

"Charlie," I said, kneeling down. I put my hand on his cheek. "Don't ever change."

He smiled and nodded.

We hugged the kids one more time and pulled away. Partings are never easy, even if they're only temporary.

As we did, I felt a painful rip in my chest. I'd never experienced anything like it, not this tugging of emotions like I had lately. But then again, I'd never met anyone like Holly and her children before. I didn't feel like the dragon I'd been before the collision. I wondered how mortal I was becoming, as though my dragon-self were disappearing without my knowledge. Would I no longer be able to change? *Was* I becoming more human? Would I forget how to fly?

I looked back at them as they stood there and put my hand in the air, hoping and praying everything would be okay.

Little did I realize . . .

—

We found Dilla-dale at the park where he said he'd be. When Karen and I flew in, smoke and fire blanketed the northern sky. The war looked roughly twenty miles away. The smell was dense, bringing tears to my eyes.

"We were able to evacuate and relocate most of the people who were staying in the area," Dilla-dale said. "Is the family safe?"

I nodded. "What should we do?"

"I feel so helpless," Dilla-dale said, exasperated. He shook his head and looked at me, trying to regain his confidence. "We're massed about fifteen miles north. They have front-line troops, tanks, even jets. I would've never thought anything like this was possible between our kind, Justin. I never would've believed it."

I wished I could do something to ease his mind.

"What do you want us to do?" I asked.

He looked at me. "I'm going to the front lines with Preston and Granger. I might be able to use my magic and thwart Lane's armies. But I'm afraid I have to volunteer you for the most dangerous task."

"Find Lane at whatever cost and try to stop her?"

"It's the only way, Justin."

I smiled. "I understand. I'm honored to be chosen."

"I'm not honored to have to ask you, but she is a dragon, and a dragon will have an advantage."

I nodded.

"And Justin?"

"Yes, Dilla-dale?"

"Cerras stirs. He's restless. Something has been unsettling me for a long time. I think he's waking up. It's going to be catastrophic when he does. Marrik is alive, his twin. This war goes beyond men and dragons, but that might be our edge."

I nodded again.

I had no plan whatsoever. Lila and Louis came with Karen and me, while Cullen remained behind in case Granger, Preston, or Dilla-dale needed him. They were frustrated, I could tell. The Old Ones and mortals would only end up getting in the way . . . or worse.

The four of us took to the sky, flying north. We were four dragons against a multitude of angry men and fire-breathing reptiles.

Fires were visible as we flew north. We sailed over the front lines, men with shields and firearms, marching forward, battling men and dragons. I saw lines of tanks, heard the cannon fire exploding on the ground. Jet planes flew overhead, making sonic booms across the sky that pained my ears. Missiles were launched. In the pandemonium, it was impossible to see who was fighting for which side.

The land around and under us was buried in smoke and fire. The shouts and screams of men were accompanied by piercing dragon cries.

The four of us descended into a land awash in death and destruction. Bodies coated the ground, and plenty of them, men and dragons. We transformed into our mortal forms when we hit the earth.

"Dear Cerras," Karen said, looking around.

Homes were burning. Trees were burning. Dragons are born from fire, but we can still be destroyed by flame.

Throughout the history of Paramis, I'd never seen anything like it. Strewn throughout the wasteland were charred corpses of men, women, and dragons, never to breathe again. I saw dragons battling one another in the air above our heads, dousing each other in flame. Dragons were on the ground, clawing and biting at each other.

One bright blue dragon on the ground struggled under ropes looped around its neck. It flapped its wings futilely, howling and crying. Five strong men, each holding tightly to a rope, their faces glistened in sweat, kept the beast on the ground while the dragon struggled, cried, and blew clouds of flame.

We were too late to save him. One man ran behind the creature and drove a long spear into its flanks. The beast cried, toppled, and fell to its side. One man retrieved a can of gasoline from a truck and poured it on the dragon's head. With torches, they set fire to it. The thing howled in agony as flames washed over him. The smell I'd noticed earlier was stronger—dragon flesh on fire. My eyes filled with tears.

Karen stood as if paralyzed, face frozen in horror. Tears spilled down her cheeks. I wasn't worried about the men. I couldn't care less. They hadn't noticed us because of the smoke. They congratulated each other, slapped one another's hands, and cheered.

"What are we supposed to do?" Louis asked.

Lane had brought this on herself, on us, and the people of Earth. I heard the futility in Louis' voice. I saw it in Karen's eyes. Lane had brought out the rage-filled demon in me. My fingers began to twitch. Lila was strangely quiet, as though trying to comprehend the magnitude of this nightmare.

Violence is not solved with violence. We are protectors, but my rage took control of me. I started toward the men.

"Justin, no!" Karen said, reaching out to pull me back, but I kept walking.

Part of me knew I would regret this. Part of me didn't care.

"Well done!" I said. They all turned toward me. "Well done!"

One of them actually smiled. I smiled in return, opening my mouth wide. I unleashed a blanket of fire, dousing all five of them at once. In seconds, their celebration turned to cries of pain. Fire encircled heads, arms, and legs. I had no idea what was going through me at that moment. Was it malice? Was it Lane's evil? Whatever it was, I hoped never to feel it again.

I watched as they ran around, screaming. Eventually, they collapsed to the ground, crisp and motionless. My behavior surprised me, like someone else taking control of my actions. I'd been reduced to this. I'd let it get the best of me.

I nodded a single time and turned back to the others.

Karen looked at me with wide eyes. I didn't say anything. Remorse was turning my heart to stone already.

More jets flew above us. Missiles were launched; cannon fire sounded. Screams and dragon cries filled the air again, the smell of smoldering flesh and dragon scales.

I watched as dragons ensnared men, biting them in two. I watched as dragons were shot and killed and beheaded. I watched in numb, disbelieving silence as the war went both ways.

Some men had built traps to waylay the dragons, which is what the five men had been doing, getting their ropes around the beasts to keep them on the ground, then attacking them with spears. In turn, dragons swooped from the sky to pluck them from the earth, taking them high into the air, then dropping them to the ground.

Shotgun blasts sounded. An indigo dragon fell, his neck erupting in a spray of blood, the blast taking out most of his throat. I hadn't thought about their weapons or firearms. My fire wouldn't stop a stray bullet. It wasn't wise for us to linger here.

Karen grabbed my arm and pointed west through the smoke and fire. "Look there," she said.

It was hard to see through the haze, but I could just make out something on the mountainside . . .

A fiery red glow was visible to the west, an illumination caused by something other than flame. It looked like the entrance to a cave, a recess on the side of the mountain three-hundred feet off the ground.

The illumination was a spectrum of colors.

I transformed and took to the sky. Karen followed. Louis and Lila were behind us. I transformed into my 'mortal' form once I reached the cave entrance. I was too enraged for caution. I hadn't thought ahead. Behind me, Karen, Louis, and Lila transformed.

The light came from several sources. Boiling magma, several hundred feet below us, reflected off diamonds, crystals, and quartz in what I thought was (despite the situation) a miraculous display of color. We stood on level ground, a solid sheet of rock widening out on either side of us. Thirty yards in, the ground ended in a cliff. Boiling magma roiled hundreds of feet below. Earth and Paramis had come together to make a cave in the bowels of a restless volcano.

Lane stood near the cliff edge, the Eye of Cerras at her feet, pulsing in kaleidoscopic glory. Lane's skin was a vortex of color, eyes alight with madness. Magma shot geysers high into the air. Tor-Latress hovered at her shoulder, a bat-like shadow without legs. He whispered in her ear, and she nodded.

Another figure was visible. My eyes were deceiving me because there was no way he could be here. The top hat, the cape, the boyish smile, and the face of a child I knew too well. Karen screamed in surprise next to me:

"CHARLIE!"

It *was* Charlie, somehow here, even though we'd left him safely with Holly moments ago. Lane had managed to kidnap him somehow, perhaps with the power of the Eye.

At the edge of the cliff, fixed to a torturous device made of wires, hooks, and metal, was Gill, Karen's brother. He was stuck in the middle of the transformation from dragon to mortal. One wounded wing bled copiously. Severe burns covered his scales. His hair was gone, singed from his head. Half his face was melted scales and skin, one eye staring blindly, red and swollen. One of his legs had failed to transform all the way.

I could only imagine what Lane must've put him through. He'd been a bright, beautiful, purple dragon at one time, full of cheer and good humor. Any semblance of his former self ended there. His skin was charred black and red with blood. I watched as he raised his head, his single eye fixing on his sister. A second later, it closed. Gill turned away.

Had she known this moment would arrive? Had she known Karen and I would find her? Had she captured and tortured Gill just to see the look in Karen's eyes?

Louis, mimicking my own anger, flew at Lane without hesitation, transforming into a dragon. He let out a single, defiant cry.

Lane turned instantly, pulling her saber from its sheath. Louis, flying toward her, breathed gouts of fire. The flames washed harmlessly over her—the power of the Eye, perhaps. Louis' couldn't stop his momentum. Lane's saber sank into his chest. His scream echoed off the cave walls.

Lila let out a scream behind me. Karen and I watched as Louis' body sagged and hit the ground.

Our fury got the better of us. We acted without thinking, a sequence of events that rushed by in a blur.

Louis blinked a single time and was still. Blood spilled over his fingers as he tried to transform. He was stuck in the middle of his change, much like Gill. Death, even though he was still alive, had stripped him of his magic.

Before I could reach out and pull Lila back, her bright yellow form raced past me toward Lane. She didn't transform into a dragon but decided to take Lane head-on. Tor-Latress halted her progress. He moved in front of Lane, protecting his master, and Lila grappled arm and arm with the shadowy demon. Wisps of black smoke spiraled around her face. To my horror, Tor-Latress—with more power than I thought him capable—forced Lila to the edge of the cliff and over the side. Lava swallowed her before she could transform.

It took all my control not to advance. If I had, I would've suffered a similar fate. Still, fury beat in my ears. Blood pumped loudly through my veins. My claws twitched with violence and murder. I'd never wanted to see another dragon suffer, but I wanted Lane to suffer then. We hadn't been in the cave for more than a minute, and already Louis and Lila were gone.

Charlie stepped back and out of the way, looking on with wide eyes. Sweat dripped from under the top hat and down his cheeks. Gill looked between the crude bars of his cage, as if simply waiting to die, ashamed of his own helplessness. I steeled my heart, thinking of Louis and Lila. Tor-Latress smiled at me with red eyes. My claws twitched again.

"Charlie," I said. "I want you to come away from there right now. Please. Come on over to me." I held out my hand to encourage him.

He cocked his head and looked at me. His face was strange. He didn't seem to recognize me. "Justin?" he said, in a robotic voice, and stepped backward again.

I turned to Lane. "What are you hoping to accomplish?"

Karen stepped beside me, locking her arm through mine. Tor-Latress turned and hissed at both of us.

Lane turned to Gill and ran her fingers along the edge of the blade, soaked in Louis' blood. "Your brother is ready to pass on to the other side, Karen," she said. "You can't blame him for his loyalty. It's admirable." She looked over at him. "Still, he's nothing more than a mongrel—the weakness of our kind. In that, he's quite pathetic."

Lane continued, looking at Charlie now: "With the power of Tor-Latress, I was able to steal Charlie from his very own dreams. He performed the ultimate magic trick, didn't you, Charlie? Stealing the Eye of Cerras—the power of shadow and light."

She smiled wide, proud of him. No doubt, she was. "We've done this before, haven't we, Charlie? Because of you and your precious magic. We will turn the hearts of men against dragons and dragons against men. We will turn dragons and men against the gods. Marrik stirs and will battle his brother. And because of the Eye, we already know the outcome. Those forces are on our side." Lane paused, still looking at Charlie. "He's a good boy. And special, too, isn't he? A magical, bright boy. Aren't you, Charlie?"

Charlie actually smiled at her. It made me ill.

"Do you think the gods are going to cooperate with you?" I asked. "Do you think they will share their power with a fool?"

Yellow eyes blazed with fire. "Marrik has promised me a throne . . . made from the bones of dead men and dragons. I will rule this new world with Tor-Latress and Charlie by my side. I couldn't do it on Paramis alone. I resurrected Tor-Latress with the power of Marrik. We're not made to be protectors, Justin. Dragons should be rulers, the way it was meant to be."

I shook my head, unable to comprehend her lunacy.

"And you think Marrik is a god of his word?"

She narrowed her eyes.

"Gill?" Karen said. She unlocked her arm with mine and stepped toward her brother.

"Why, Gill?" I asked. "Why, in the name of Cerras, would you torture him, Lane? He's one of our own kind."

Lane shrugged as if it didn't matter to her one way or the other. "We are not evolving. We have become weak. Protecting the likes of the Old Ones and mortals. We rule our own destiny, Justin Silas.

We are not slaves to these beings. We are dragons! Beasts! We are born from fire, not guardians. We are rulers of the skies and stars. *We* are the root of all magic!" She turned and smiled at Charlie.

"Lane," I said, knowing my words would be useless here. The influence of Tor-Latress and the Eye was working through her. "I beg you! Don't do this!"

She ignored me.

"Charlie has a special gift," she said, looking at him with maternal love. "I knew about him all along. Even on Paramis. He's a boy who resounds with magic. Cerras must've granted him something special. I will raise Marrik to destroy his brother. When that happens, mortals will cease to exist. Anyone who opposes Marrik will suffer death by fire. Cerras will be gone, and all will be as it should've been in the beginning. Dragons will rule once more. You'll see how infantile all this has been, how futile your cause. *We* are the ones to rule the Old Ones. This is what we've been driving toward since the beginning of time. Dragons have always been more powerful than men. I'm here to remind them of that fact. Bow to the rule or suffer the consequences. You can join me, Justin Silas of Amberlye . . . or you can die. There is no third option."

Dilla-dale had mentioned a twin. In my mind's eye, I saw another war, one playing itself out in the frozen regions to the north. In a blinding, white, wind-blown landscape, two giants made of precious stones grappled arm in arm, endeavoring to overthrow the other. Cerras and Marrik were twins, but they were mortal enemies.

Karen, as carefully as she could, began to move toward Charlie. I wondered how long the boy had been under Lane's spell. I wondered why he hadn't told us about his dreams . . . that he'd known about Lane all along. The Eye had great power, and its influence—along with Tor-Latress—was playing a role.

I reached for Karen, wondering what plan she had in mind, one that excluded me because she didn't have the chance to tell me. She was taking a risk, saw an opening, and was acting on it.

"Lane, *please,*" I said. "I'm begging you. This is *madness!*"

"That's what makes you so pathetic, Justin," she said. "That you're a dragon, and you still have the weakness to plead."

Lane shook her head, holding the saber by her side.

I saw Gill and Karen's eyes lock. Gill nodded a single time. Karen kept her chin firm and nodded. I saw tears pouring down her cheeks. They'd made a silent pact.

Gill said something to Lane I didn't hear. He turned and laughed loudly at her expense. It was enough. She kicked Gill's cage as hard as she could, sending him over the edge and into the magma. As she did, Karen bolted for Charlie.

I had to move fast. Karen was already ahead of me, tears fueling her eyes.

There was sureness on Gill's face before he plummeted to his death. It was the opportunity Karen needed. Lane had paused too long, watching Gill fall into the magma. Karen reached out and grabbed Charlie's hand, pulling him toward her. Lane saw it out of the corner of her eye and turned around.

Tor-Latress whipped his head in Karen's direction, hissing violently. His form darted over her head, preventing her from getting Charlie out of the cave. Retreating with him as Gill was sent over the edge had been her plan. To my horror, I realized this, too, had failed.

My only hope was to advance and catch Lane off guard, to face her, Tor-Latress, and the power of the Eye on my own.

The cliff trembled.

I saw in my mind Cerras and his brother battling through landscapes of blue ice again.

I ran forward. Everything was moving too fast.

Or too slow.

Karen's foot kicked out because of Tor-Latress. She stuck the Eye of Cerras, sending it over the edge and out of sight.

When I'd first seen Charlie in the cave, thinking my eyes were playing tricks on me, I saw something similar now.

Carl Underhill materialized out of nowhere, his face a mask of fury. He stood on the cliff's platform several feet from Lane.

Tor-Latress shrieked and hissed, looking frantic. His eyes smoldered with rage, trying to decide what to do: fend me off as I advanced or defend his master?

Karen grabbed Charlie's hand and hurried back toward the cave entrance as Tor-Latress unraveled himself from her head. In the same instant, Lane reached out and grabbed Karen's arm, holding her back. Carl, somehow, with physicality—even as a ghost—

rushed forward with arms extended to push Lane over and into the magma.

But that's not what happened.

Carl didn't realize Lane had grabbed Karen's arm until it was too late. Karen, in her panic, thought only of holding onto Charlie to keep him safe.

I, Justin Silas of Amberlye, wasn't quick enough in *any* light.

I reached them all too late . . .

Carl succeeded in driving Lane over the edge, but she took Karen and Charlie with her. All three descended into the magma in a horrifying chain.

I screamed, reaching out. Everything was moving too fast. My fingers brushed the fabric of Charlie's cape, but that was.

I braced myself, falling onto my stomach. I skidded to a stop before sailing over the edge. I reached out, shrieking as Karen, Charlie, and Lane were swallowed by the magma. Tears sprang to my eyes. I wailed Karen's name. I watched, helpless, as they splashed into the lava.

Dragon tears spilled down my face.

In seconds, the scene had unfolded. In seconds, it was over. Lane was dead. Karen was gone.

And Cerras help me, so was Charlie.

I was too stunned to think. I thought about Holly and how I was going to explain this.

I turned and stood up, numb with shock.

I looked at Carl, tears blurring my eyes. His face pleaded with me, begging forgiveness. His eyes were wide, holding his hands up. He shook his head. He was just as surprised and horrified, his look told me. He didn't speak a word. I wondered if he could.

Carl looked to the side and over the edge. He shook his head, looked back at me, and fell to his knees. He buried his ghostly hands to his face and wept without making a sound.

I'd lost my one true love.

Carl, for a second time, had lost a son.

I'd forgotten about Cerras and the magic Eye. It, too, had fallen into the magma. The trembling I'd felt earlier was now a violent rumble under my feet, shaking the inside of the volcano. Pillars of molten, orange liquid rocketed into the air.

I thought of staying. What had I to live for? But Tor-Latress shrieked, bringing me out of my grief. That shadow was still alive. Rage consumed me, and I turned to face the demon.

In my mind once more, I saw the struggle between two massive giants. One fell backward, blanketed in snow. I couldn't tell if it was Marrik or Cerras.

In the next second, I got my answer.

A massive hand made of diamonds emerged from the magma. It closed around Tor-Latress. It crushed the shadow into a lifeless pulp and retreated again.

It was small satisfaction.

I had seconds before the mountain exploded. The walls continued to shake. I looked at Carl. He was still on his knees. His palms were up, face wet with tears, begging my forgiveness.

But what can you say to a ghost?

I shook my head, trying to tell him it wasn't his fault. It had been an accident. He'd meant well. It was just an accident.

I transformed, took to the air, and flapped my wings as hard as I could, retreating from the cave and into the smoky sky.

The mountainside exploded behind me. A shower of lava, flame, and rock hurled me, senseless, three-hundred feet below.

9.

His Hand in Mine

Dilla-dale is schooling Mellicent and Jody in the history of New Earth and Paramis Altered. They've taken solace in helping—with the aid of a little magic—to rebuild Dilla-dale's tower. Dilla-dale is very happy about this, and he's taken to the children as teachers will take to their students.

Mellicent and Jody have graduated from Stage One. They both wear white robes now, novices in the endless instruction of eternal wisdom and magic. They look good in the robes, too, I admit, much better than those silly, unfashionable Earth-garments they used to wear. The robes were a pleasant gift from the Old Ones, and they enjoy them immensely. They're good kids, and they're growing wiser and taller as the days go by. Mellicent can hold stones and make them twirl in circles above her palm, much to Jody's chagrin. Jody will learn this trick as well, and there will be magical competitions between the two sisters in the days ahead.

With the destruction of the Eye of Cerras (much to my surprise), the world did *not* fall into pandemonium as I'd expected.

Lane's influence vanished, along with Tor-Latress.

There are survivors, but with Lane's defeat, dragons and mortals are no longer at war.

When I returned to the cabin after the destruction of the mountain, Holly, Mellicent, and Jody knew what happened right away. Five of us had gone away, including Charlie. And I, Justin Silas, was the only one to return. I didn't *want* to return. I didn't want to be the one to tell them what happened, add more sorrow to what was already a difficult time for everyone.

Lila was gone, along with Louis. Karen and Charlie were gone. I held onto Holly for a long time, and we wept in our grief. We'd lost some beautiful people in the short time we'd known each other.

I told Holly that Carl had helped in destroying Lane. I told her all I could while leaving out the more horrifying aspects of how Gill looked and what really happened to Louis and Lila. It was the hardest thing I'd ever had to tell anyone . . . that her Charlie was gone, her little Harry Houdini.

Things are quieter now. I suppose that's a good thing. I'm not sure. We have no choice but to find some peace and harmony where two planets, races, and cultures once existed. We are forced to become one.

Maybe things will mend themselves in time. I don't know. But it's good to have something to hope for.

We're still in the cabin, despite its cramped size. I stay with Holly, watching over her, Mellicent, and Jody while helping Dilladale in any way I can.

We haven't lost everything, I tell myself. We've gained a lot. I try to remind myself of this, but it's hard.

I no longer have the power to transform. I'm not sure why. I'm a seven-foot reptile without wings. Somehow, with the destruction of Cerras' Eye, I've lost my ability to change. I always thought my true nature was to have wings instead of legs. Being a dragon is what makes me who I am. But for some reason, that particular talent is gone. I can no longer breathe fire, either.

Perhaps this world is making me mortal after all.

Life goes on . . .

The Eyes of Cerras are everywhere. Lights are visible. In some aspects, I wonder if it was Cerras' plan all along—far outweighing Lane's. I don't think his Eye was destroyed, and I don't think Cerras is completely gone.

I believe there's more magic in the world than I can comprehend.

Stars randomly spot the landscape, shedding light for all to see. They are Cerras watching over us. I don't know how I know that, but I do. They're bright and plentiful. If I could fly again, I would take to the sky, soaring under the clouds, and see the way the world looks, replete with that magnificent silvery-blue illumination. It must be a glorious sight!

The days pass, and spring turns to summer. Our grief and loss heal with the passing of time. It's been a trial since the collision, too much for words, but we make the best of it.

We had another rally, a meeting with Granger, Preston, Dilladale, and Murrochoe. It proved much different with Lane's demise. Riots didn't follow, much to everyone's relief. Murrochoe was how I remembered him: ancient, but his eyes are white and silver now.

He made a brief appearance and went into isolation again. I was surprised Dilla-dale didn't follow, but he's needed, and despite what he says, being an active participant in the community does him good. Even if he grumbles about it.

One late sunny afternoon in summer, I was sitting outside on the porch swing with Holly beside me. Holly and I had put the swing together earlier that week, fixing it with chains above the porch where the roof extended. We enjoyed spending the afternoons sitting on it and watching the sun go down. I always think my weight will pull the screws out, and I'll break my tailbone, but so far, it's held.

The passing of Lane, Karen, Gill, and Charlie was three months behind us. Grief does not pass so quickly. Lane would be pleased with our suffering, and I didn't like the idea of giving her any victory.

Mellicent and Jody were outside with us. They sat on the steps of the porch playing a game Dilla-dale had taught them using magic stones and small branches from ancient trees. It was supposed to relax and stimulate the mind at the same time. They looked wise and older in their white robes, but they were still teenage girls.

Dilla-dale had given them some time off to ponder the deeper complexities of life. His tower was finished, a labor that had taken some amount of time, but he was happier having a place to study again. We visit him sometimes, always interrupting him as he pores over ancient volumes at his desk. He's been enjoying history books about Earth, fascinated with George Washington and Abraham Lincoln. He says Lincoln, although melancholy, was an astounding figure.

One day, he approached Holly with a thick tome in his hand and said, "Who is this Jesus Christ fella? Boy, would I like to meet him!" Holly laughed for a long time while Dilla-dale and I looked at each other and shrugged.

While we were sitting on the porch swing, a beige-colored Cadillac pulled into the driveway. This was rare. We didn't see many people driving cars anymore since gasoline was scarce. Some of the power grids had been rerouted and restored, and electricity was working in some parts of the neighborhood again. This made Holly very happy. She was able to return to an old love of cooking and baking, which she did often. I still don't know the names of the pastries she makes, but they are savory, sweet, and delicious.

We looked up. Granger was sitting behind the steering wheel. Someone else was sitting in the back of the car, but I couldn't make out who it was.

The driver's side door opened. The sun gleamed off the chrome bumper and windows. Granger smiled, his teeth bright under his dark skin. His black hair reflected the sun in that spiky, spongy way.

"Greetings," he said, cheerfully. "You guys in the mood for a visitor?"

I raised my eyebrows and looked at Holly. She looked at me and shrugged.

"Sure," she said, turning back to Granger.

Granger nodded, smiling. He seemed pleased with himself. He went to the back door and opened it. The figure stepped out onto the driveway.

Or *did* it?

I wasn't sure what I was looking at. My heart surged, a swell of emotion. My eyes were playing tricks on me, which they seemed to be doing a lot lately.

Magic is a strange thing. Despite where I've come from, it still surprises me.

The top hat rose above the car door, and I saw the cape unfurl.

Beside me, Holly gasped. Her hands went to her face.

Something wasn't right, though, something unnatural . . .

It *was* Charlie. Of course, it was. Who else could it be?

But when Granger shut the door and the boy stood there, I heard the life go out of Holly. It *was* cruel, whatever it was, and I wondered what Granger was thinking by doing this.

I looked at the mayor again. He was smiling wide, and I realized this wasn't a joke.

It was the top hat and cape, but other than these two articles of clothing, there was nothing there. The boy—his *flesh,* his face— were invisible. The top hat and cape moved all by themselves.

We were looking at a ghost.

Holly began to cry. Mellicent and Jody stood up from the porch steps. When I looked at them, they were smiling like Granger was, knowing something Holly and I did not.

Charlie walked up to Holly and me, his cape unfurling around his ankles. An elegant magician, he'd somehow acquired a shiny black cane. As his steps indicated, he was using it perfectly, twirling it with grace. His stride—although I couldn't see his legs or feet—was gallant as he walked. The cane twirled in invisible hands.

He stopped before the porch swing, his hat turning one way, then the other, looking at me, then at Holly.

"Howdy gang," his voice emerged from a non-existent face.

Or *was* it non-existent?

Holly went pale. She was crying, overjoyed, wondering why Charlie was here. Was this only a visit? Was this his ghost, a last parting magic trick? Or was it some cruel joke from Cerras?

"Why is everyone so glum?" he asked.

I wanted to reach out and touch him, but I resisted.

"Charlie?" Holly said. "Is that really you?"

"Of *course* it's me, Mom," he said. "Jeez! Don't you recognize your own kid when you see him?"

Mellicent and Jody laughed.

"Hey, Charlie," Mellicent said.

"Yeah," Jody said. "What's up, Charlie? Where have you *been?*"

The top of the cape, where it rolled over his shoulders, moved upwards in an invisible shrug. "Well," he said. "Not all magic tricks are so easy. The hand is quicker than Cerras' Eye." Charlie giggled to himself.

Holly reached out and touched him. It was the weirdest thing I'd ever seen. I watched her fingers curl around his invisible arms. I watched her mouth kiss an invisible cheek. It was Charlie. How could it *not* be? He was here. He was solid. He just wasn't . . . *visible.*

"It's really you," Holly said. "How did you do it? How come you're here? How come we can't *see* you?"

"Part of the process, I think," Charlie said. "Cerras told me it might come back in time, but even *he* wasn't completely sure. I think he just likes to test me. Unlike *you,"* he said, his hat turning in my direction.

Feeling ridiculous, I found myself talking to the hat and not to the face underneath it. "What do you mean?" I asked.

"You can fly," Charlie said. "You just haven't tried hard enough."

"Don't, Charlie," I said. "It's not polite to play with a dragon's feelings."

"Who's playing?" he said. "If you *can't* fly, I can *make* you fly. I'm magic, you know? Cerras says so. He says I'm going to be a great magician someday."

I had no idea how to respond to this. Holly, too, was speechless. Granger approached slowly, not sure what to do with himself. He leaned against one of the wooden beams of the porch. He nodded in my direction and folded his arms.

"Mom?" Charlie said.

I still couldn't get over how his voice emerged from thin air.

"Yeah?" she asked.

"Can I sit with Justin for a minute? I need to talk to him. The old boy has a lot to learn, but I think I can help him."

Holly actually laughed and stood up. "Of course, honey. Do you want me to leave you two alone for a while?"

"No," Charlie said. "That won't be necessary. Unless you want to."

I looked down the block. Not surprising me, Carl stood in the middle of the road, looking in our direction. Our eyes met. He wore the black jacket and white shirt. He held his palms up and shrugged. 'It was the best I could do,' he seemed to say. I nodded in reply, and that's when the tears came. I was starting to feel like Holly lately . . . how she cried all the time.

Carl smiled, chuckled to himself, and raised his hand in my direction. He nodded, turned, and put his hands in his pockets. He looked up at the sky and actually squinted at the brightness of the sun. I watched his lips purse, whistling a silent tune to himself.

Holly walked over and put her arms around her daughters' shoulders. Charlie sat next to me on the porch swing. His weight made it creak. I felt his feet kicking out rhythmically, even though I couldn't see them.

"Justin," he told me. All the humor and good nature went out of his voice. He was very serious. "Karen wanted me to bring you something."

I wasn't sure how much more of this I could take. Karen was gone. I knew that. I felt it. Despite having Charlie there, he wasn't *really* there, was he? This was just a cruel trick.

Like the magician he was, a bundle of antique-colored envelopes appeared out of nowhere. They were wrapped in string. He placed them on my lap. In elegant script—script I recognized as Karen's—was my name on the one on top.

"She wanted me to give these to you, Justin," Charlie said. "She wanted me to tell you that she loves you and that she's always with you. That there's more magic in the world now than ever before, and that anything is possible . . . as long as you just believe."

I sobbed. How could I not? Holly grabbed Jody and Mellicent and steered them inside. Granger followed, turning once to smile at me before the screen shut behind him. Holly thought it best to give us some time alone.

"Thank you, Charlie," I said, staring down at the letters. They were heavy, bundles of pages. I couldn't wait to read them. I wondered when she'd written them. I wondered many things. For now, I would wait. It was something very personal, something I wanted to savor in my own time. I held the envelopes against my chest and took a deep breath.

For a second, a strange light emanated from under the top hat. I felt Charlie's hand grab mine. It was solid, small, the hand of a nine-year-old boy. I felt each individual finger curl around my own. He squeezed.

"That's from Karen," Charlie said. "She wanted me to let you know. 'Squeeze his hand for me, Charlie,' she said. 'And tell him it's from me.'"

I couldn't stop crying. I held my hands to my face, shedding dragon tears. I blubbered like a seven-foot, two-inch-tall, fiery-skinned idiot. It was silent, but it was a good cry, and I could feel Karen. I could smell her hair.

"I love you, Charlie," I said. "I love you so much. I don't know how to thank you for this. It's the best gift anyone has ever given me."

I saw his shoulders shrug. He squeezed my hand again.

"It's nothing," he said.

We sat in silence on the porch swing for some time. A cool breeze made the summer day virtually perfect. Charlie didn't let go of my hand as we sat there. It was a private moment shared between an ageless dragon and an undying child.

According to Charlie, nothing *had* changed. I was a dragon still and always would be.

I heard Granger laugh from inside.

The sun was beginning to set, sending colors and stars of light across the sky. It was turning into a beautiful evening.

I've heard the icy regions of Canastelle still exist up north. They've come to life here on New Earth and Paramis Altered. I hear the Forests of Glammis breed fairy-folk, but those are just rumors, tales to excite children across Delayne and America both. I wonder if some of those old cities still exist and if that ancient architecture still tugs at my heartstrings like it used to. I haven't flown for a while, but I'm assuming there's a lot left to see. I'm anxious to fly again, too, and it's good to know that no matter how much I miss Paramis, that magical land still exists. It comes to life more each day, and I think it adds to the beauty of Earth without taking away its own magic. That's one of the many things to be thankful for now.

After a long time, Charlie asked:

"So, when do you plan on taking me flying, Justin Silas of Amberlye?"

I laughed through my tears. "Does this mean you plan on hanging around for a while?" I asked.

"What do *you* think?" he said.

I turned and looked at him. For the briefest instant, the quickest second, I saw his face, his gleaming, exuberant youth emanating visibly from under the top hat. He turned to look at me and winked, and it was *not* my imagination. It was very real. Charlie's lips curled upward, revealing the hint, the ghost of a smile.

I laughed out loud.

Of all the tricks he performed, this one, to me—the most simple—transcended them all.

I realized I was in the presence of greatness . . .

And I have a feeling I'll be here for a while still . . .

Thanks for coming along for the ride, Dear Reader.
Reviews are always appreciated, especially if you liked the tale.

Enjoy these other titles and genres by Brandon Berntson:

Horror:
Hill Haven Creeps and the Halloween King
Snapdragon
Boone
Corona of Blue

Collections:
Darkness and Devotion: Tales of Horror, Fantasy, and Romance
Body of Immorality: Tales of Madness and the Macabre

The Lovecraft Mysteries:
The Night of Dagon (The Lovecraft Mysteries Book 1)
Arkham: Reanimated (The Lovecraft Mysteries Book 2)
The Lurker at the Threshold (the Lovecraft Mysteries Book 3)

The Trilogy of Blood and Fire:
All The Gods Against Me (Book I)
Calliope (Book II)
Worlds Away (Book III)
The Trilogy of Blood and Fire Box Set

Young Adult Fantasy:
When We Were Dragons
Castle Juliet

Comedy/Horror:
Buick Cannon: (A Joke from the Moon)

Brandon Berntson studied English and Literature at Utah State University but grew up in various towns throughout Colorado, where most of his stories take place. His work spans from serious, adult horror to playful, young adult fantasy and everything in between. He is the author of *Castle Juliet* and *When We Were Dragons,* enchanting, magical reads for all ages. He is also the author of *Body of Immorality*, a cryptic collection of horror stories, and the raw, adult-themed, *All The Gods Against Me.*

Brandon is a fan of Stephen King, Clive Barker, Ramsey Campbell, Jonathan Carroll, Anne Rice, Elizabeth Hand, Peter Straub, and classic literature.

He enjoys Colorado sports, Bugs Bunny, Beethoven, Ronnie James Dio, *The X-files,* and classic horror films. He makes his home in Boulder, Colorado.

Follow him on:
Twitter
Facebook
Facebook Author Page

Join the mailing list and get updates free at
www.brandonberntson.com

Made in the USA
Las Vegas, NV
26 October 2021